A novel
based on the
legend of

KE*R*RIVAN

the Society of
Masterless Men

A novel
based on the
legend of

KERRIVAN

the Society of
Masterless Men

ELDON DRODGE

jesperson
publishing

jesperson
publishing

100 Water Street
P. O. Box 2188
St. John's, NL
A1C 6E6

National Library of Canada Cataloguing in Publication Data

Drodge, Eldon 1942-
Kerrivan: A novel based on the legend of the Society of Masterless Men

ISBN 0-921692-98-6
I. Title.
PS8557.R62K47 2001   C813'.6   C2001-901702-2
PR9199.3.D76K47 2001

Design/Layout:

Printed in Canada.

Dedicated to my three grandsons,
Daniel, Zachary, and Benjamin.

Thanks to my wife, Joan, and daughter, Susan,
for all their help and support, and all the people
who read my first publication, JACKMAN, and
encouraged me to write another.

one

The scene unfolding on the deck of the *H.M.S. Fortress* was in sharp contrast to the beauty of the morning. Only a scattering of white cloud far distant in the west interrupted the vast expanse of clear blue sky that otherwise stretched unbroken from horizon to horizon. The large four-masted frigate ploughed gently westward through a moderately rolling sea, pushed by a fair southeast wind that filled her huge sails just enough to cant her slightly to starboard as she slipped effortlessly onward toward her destination. Although it was still early in the morning, many of the men on board had stripped themselves to the waist to feel the unseasonably warm sun and the caress of the gentle breeze on their bodies that would normally be wrapped in layers of clothing to ward off the cold dampness that marked most mornings on the Atlantic Ocean at this time of year. It was one of those rare spring days that men at sea have savored since the beginning of time.

The rails of the *Fortress* were lined with the full complement of her one-hundred and twenty man crew. Also present were the forty prisoners that the large naval ship carried, all being transported to Newfoundland and America. Every man on board, officers, crewmen and prisoners alike, had been summoned out to witness the flogging of the three men who stood tied and shackled before the ship's master silently awaiting their punishment. Each of the sentenced men hoped fervently for the last-minute reprieve that they knew in their innermost beings would never come. At the very least they hoped to be given not more than the standard half dozen lashes usually administered for minor transgressions and misdemeanors.

But it was not to be. Captain Joshua Smith, the man who had ordered the floggings and who was now standing by to see his instructions carried out by his senior officers, felt compelled to make an example of the three men. The *Fortress* was only three days out of her home port of Plymouth and still had a very long way to go. Past experience told him that it was better to lay down the law early than to show leniency that might lead to other more serious offenses later in the voyage.

Thus, the ship's officers, her crew, and her human cargo of murderers, thieves and felons of every kind all stood in silence and waited for the floggings to commence.

The first of the three men to be led to the mast was small in stature. His wiry body seemed to resist the short walk to the flogging post with a will of its own and he had to be propelled forward by the two guards who held him on each side. The stark fear that he felt inside showed plainly on his pockmarked face as his eyes darted furtively over the assembled men before coming to rest on the face of Captain Smith, mutely pleading for mercy. He knew what was coming. He had been flogged before.

At the Captain's nod, the officer gave the order for the punishment to begin. Except for the loud grunt that punctuated each stroke of the lash, the man bore the first two lashes surprisingly well. The scream that issued forth on the third and each succeeding stroke, however, came from the very depths of his being until, on the fourteenth stroke, he finally passed out. The pain of the last six strokes administered to his unconscious body still obviously registered somewhere deep within him as his body jerked and twitched spasmodically with each blow.

The second man, who was much bigger and heavier than the first, towering well over six feet with extremely broad sloping shoulders, did better. He walked without hesitation to the mast, his brooding eyes fastened on Captain Smith in a belligerent stare of hatred and defiance even as his feet and wrists were being bound to the whipping post to ensure that he would be totally immobilized while his punishment was being inflicted. When someone among the onlookers snickered, he glared at the assemblage, trying to ascertain who it was. Unable to do so, he bared his teeth and snarled at them all.

"Damn your eyes, the bloody lot of you. I'll see you all in hell someday, and then, by God, I'll have my turn." He did not cry out until the tenth stroke, and remained conscious for all but the last two.

Finally, the third man was led forward. Unlike the other prisoners lining the rail, whose bodies and faces almost to a man showed the ravages of years of violence and debasement, this man was clearly different. Standing erect before his tormentors, naked save for the once-white but now torn and bloodstained breeches that he wore, it was evident that, other than the fresh cuts and bruises on his face and head, no other previous scar or blemish marred any part of his well-proportioned and muscular body. In a different setting he might have been considered handsome.

As Smith looked into the face of the tall man before him, the piercing blue eyes that stared back at him seemed to penetrate into the Captain's very soul. The man's blond hair and the intensity of his blue eyes suggested that some of the Teutonic blood of the fierce Saxons who had invaded and taken England four hundred years earlier still flowed in his veins. In his forty years as an officer in His Majesty's Royal Navy, Smith had seen only a handful of men like this one before – unyielding, uncompromising, unbending, and possessed of some powerful inner force that would never let him bow to authority no matter how frequent or how severe the punishment.

Despite the many floggings and other forms of punishment that he had administered over the years, Smith, now sixty-one years of age, was at heart a kind and Christian man, and had extracted no measure of pleasure from any of these occurrences. Epitomizing the British penchant for order and discipline, he simply saw the floggings as his duty to the King and country that he had always so faithfully served. Sadly, he recognized that in more charitable circumstances, the man now facing him might have aspired to some significant accomplishment or perhaps even greatness. The handful of men in whom he had sensed this extraordinary inner strength had, unfortunately, either by choice or through the strange twists and turns of fate, been hardened criminals by the time he had come face to face with them on the decks of his ships.

The first stroke of the lash laid the man's back open to the bone. The man wielding the whip, who was by now himself sweating profusely with the effort of his exertions, was an expert at his job. He knew how to, with a subtle roll of his wrist at the last instant, make the knotted ends of the cat-o-nine-tails strike individually in rapid succession, rather than all at once, thus causing the instrument of pain to bite as deeply as possible and to inflict the maximum agony, yet somehow never leaving the recipients permanently maimed except for the scars that most of them would carry to their graves. Oddly, like Captain Smith, he too had taken no particular pleasure from the dozens of floggings that he had given over the years. He had always considered it to be just a part of his job on the *Fortress* and simply took pride in his work. It was known that on more than one occasion he had afterwards visited the ship's infirmary to offer whatever little comfort and solace he could to some poor devil to whom he had only hours before applied the lash.

The blond man had promised himself that he wouldn't give them the satisfaction of hearing him scream. But like the others, by the tenth or twelfth stroke he too was screaming and cursing. Yet never once did he beg for mercy during the entire excruciating ordeal. Unlike the others, however, he did not pass out. He bore his full punishment of twenty-five lashes, five more than the other two men had received, in total, merciless consciousness. The look of venomous hatred that he cast toward Smith at the end as he was being led away to the infirmary, defiant and unrepentant still, sent an involuntary chill through the ship's master, and Smith, despite himself, averted his eyes. A sudden feeling of unease pervaded the Captain's thoughts as he dismissed the assembled crew and ordered the prisoners back to their confinement.

The intended deterrent effect of being forced to watch the floggings of the three men was lost on the majority of the prisoners who had been assembled for the spectacle. They had all seen it before. Most of them were too hardened by the violence and brutality of their own lives to even care anymore. Only a few still retained enough compassion and decency to feel some small shred of sympathy for the poor devils who had just been flogged. Even then, some of the sympathy that they felt was perhaps as much reserved for themselves as for the three victims, knowing that the next time it might be they themselves on the receiving end of the lash. A few others in whom the capacity for compassion or any other form of goodwill toward another human being had long since been eradicated, could scarcely keep the perverse and sadistic pleasure that they felt at the sight of flayed flesh and running blood from showing plainly on their faces.

two

For two full days he drifted in and out of consciousness. He fought the excruciating pain that racked his body and numbed his mind, willing himself to stay awake until the agony became utterly unbearable and then, despite his struggle, he would feel himself slipping into the oblivion that would give him a few moments of temporary relief. When he was awake he could hardly breathe. The overwhelming stench of vomit, blood, and the other foul smells that flooded the infirmary were suffocating him. The shaft of light entering through the small window of the infirmary, not much more than a narrow vertical slot in the wall, stung his eyes and sent sharp lightning jolts through his pain-racked brain. Twice he had tried to move closer to the tiny opening to get more air. Each time his feeble attempt had failed and he had immediately fallen back as the pain of the effort of movement overwhelmed him. He had lost all track of time. When he opened his eyes again only blackness filled the room, and he knew that it was night. The small slot in the wall now mercifully permitted a little more of the cool night air to enter the room and he was able to breathe a little easier.

His mind was a tumbled confusion of thoughts and images in which fantasy and reality merged and became inseparable, indistinguishable from one another. At one moment he was running joyfully through the lush green meadows of his childhood village of Lifford, his bare feet flying over the ground and his laughter echoing through the surrounding hillside, or splashing once again in the cool waters of the gentle River Foyle as he had done almost every day as a boy. The next moment he was fleeing through a dark, grimy street trying desperately to outrun the taloned hands that stretched out from behind to grab him. When the glowering face of Captain

Smith swam before his eyes, he instinctively reached out to rake it with his fingernails, but when he did, the disembodied image transformed itself into the grinning face of his father whom he hadn't seen in more than seventeen years. He wasn't even aware that the ship's physician had been in twice to apply a dressing of goose grease to his bloodied and shredded back.

Even in the darkness, he could tell that the whimpering and sobbing of the man in the cot to his left came from John Styles. He had only known Styles a short while, less than a year, and had detested the small, ferret-faced man from the moment he had first met him. He had immediately recognized the vile little man for what he was – an informer and a snitch. In the shadowy subculture of the criminal underworld, a snitch like Styles ranked very close to the bottom of the hierarchy, scorned and reviled by all others. He walked a precarious and danger-ous line, managing to survive only by his stealth and cunning, relying on the protection of the wardens and guards responsible for his safety. But even they, despite the fact that they were the ones who benefitted most from the information supplied to them, were known to have occasionally looked the other way while some well-deserving snitch was being punished by other prisoners as they exacted their revenge upon him.

The loud snoring that came from someone on his right was punctuated at frequent intervals by loud grunts and groans. Its familiarity told him that Ned Finn was also lying somewhere close to him in the infirmary. Finn, to whom he owed a great debt of gratitude, was one of the few true friends he had ever known, and he knew that he would follow the big, burly, kindhearted man into the very fires of hell if he had to. He fervently hoped that Finn wasn't suffering too greatly from his flogging.

He also knew that somewhere in the darkness of the infir-mary there was someone else. He could tell by the rattle of tortured breathing that the man, whoever he was, was probably drawing his last breaths.

Slightly revived by the cooler night air, he tried to make some sense of the events that had landed him in this sorry state. His status on the *Fortress* lay strangely somewhere between that of a full-fledged member of His Majesty's Royal

Navy and that of a prisoner. Of the forty men who had boarded the ship in chains three days earlier, only he and two others, because of their unique circumstances, had not been confined to the oversized brig that had originally been built to house enemy soldiers captured during skirmishes at sea. Instead he and the other two men had been allowed to freely roam the length and breadth of the ship, albeit under the scrutiny of a ship's officer or some crewman most of the time. Given no particular instructions, they were told to be ready and available for duty if and when they were requested to do so. At no time, however, had he or either of the other two men ever been ordered to do anything.

The problem had started late in the afternoon on the previous day as the prisoners were being led under guard in small groups of seven or eight up on the deck for a few minutes of fresh air and exercise as prescribed by the regulations of His Majesty's Royal Navy. He had seen Styles, who lagged behind the others, whisper conspiratorially into the ear of one of the guards. Presumably on the basis of whatever Styles had told him, the guard had immediately singled out Finn and began to question and harass him in a very vociferous manner. Whatever had been said so inflamed and enraged the huge prisoner that he had thrust the guard aside as if he were a rag doll, taken Styles into his huge manacled hands and shaken him like a terrier with its prey. The small man's obvious attempt to ingratiate himself with his captors had clearly backfired on him as he squealed and screamed helplessly in the big man's iron grip.

It took the four guards who went to Styles's rescue several minutes to bring Finn down. They rained blow after blow on his head and body until the big man finally went to his knees. Although he was fallen, bloodied and dazed, they did not let up in their punishment and continued to pummel the now defenseless man.

The blond man had watched the entire proceedings. At the sight of his friend, Finn, being battered into insensibility, he could resist no longer and had jumped into the fray without giving any thought to the consequences of his actions. In the melee that ensued, he had lashed out with wild abandon, striking at anyone who came near, until the truncheon that he didn't see coming sent him into swirling blackness.

And now, as he lay in the foul darkness of the infirmary, paying dearly for his intervention, he had not a moment's regret for having tried to come to the aid of his friend. He did, however, bemoan whatever new fate must now surely await him.

three

He was a product of the streets of Dublin. For almost seven years, from the time he was ten until he was well into his sixteenth year, he survived in the dirty, rat-infested lanes and back alleys of Ireland's oldest, largest, and grimiest city among the teeming masses of humanity that inhabited its bustling east end. The only lasting memory of his life prior to that time was the endless physical abuse of an alcoholic father who had beaten him mercilessly almost every day, ceasing only when the man's depraved need to inflict pain was satisfied for the moment. His mother, whose face he could no longer envisage, had been unable to stop the abuse; indeed, she and her other two children had been just as much victims as he himself was of the cruel and sadistic man whom they had the misfortune to have as the head of their household.

Finally, unable to endure the constant torture any longer, he had run away from home. Over a period of almost three weeks, during which he foraged for food and water in farmers' fields by day and slept at night curled up under some tree or behind some fence, he had gradually made the long journey to Dublin on the southeast coast of the country. The overwhelming grayness of the city, its cramped buildings, strange smells, unceasing clamor, and its bustling hordes of people were a far cry from the pastoral countryside he had known at Lifford, a sleepy little village a hundred and twenty miles to the north in the County Donegal. He was frightened and intimidated by his new surroundings. Yet, although homeless with nobody to turn to for comfort or the necessities of life but instilled with natural wariness and a strong instinct for survival, he quickly integrated into the sad and seedy underworld that the more well-to-do citizens of the great city knew little or nothing about.

Within a week of his arrival in Dublin, he was an accepted member of a band of seven boys who ranged in age from eight to thirteen, children already hardened beyond their years to the grim realities of life on the streets. They had spotted him during one of his blatantly inexperienced attempts to steal a piece of fruit from a vendor's stall, and knew instinctively that he was new to the streets. Having never seen him in the area before, they realized that he did not yet belong to any other rival band and that his addition would give them increased strength in numbers, something vital to their everyday existence. It was more family than he had ever known. The boys cared for each other, shared what little food or clothing they had, and protected and looked after each other as best they could in their pitiful circumstances. At night they took shelter in an abandoned shed that they had discovered behind one of the derelict houses that lined the back-alley known as Osbern's Blind. The small decrepit outbuilding, obviously used at one time to house hens or rabbits, or perhaps a pig or two, still reeked of the ingrained leavings of its original occupants as well as many years of rot and decay. It leaked badly when it rained, and rats, mice, and other vermin shared the space with them. But it was shelter.

The boys gathered there each night, had their own special sleeping places within the structure, and kept a vigilant eye throughout the night for intruders. Having once been forced from their previous shelter by a gang of older boys who had burst in upon them during the night and sent them fleeing into the streets, they didn't want the same thing to happen to them again. They also relied on each other to avoid the dangers of other gangs, predators and perverts and, above all else, the policemen whom they feared most of all.

The one factor that survival on the streets depended on more than anything else was their ability to steal without being caught. And, whether working alone or in groups, they were all experts. Never totally free of the gnawing pain of hunger, the boys often consumed whatever morsels of food they were able to lay their hands on immediately on the spot where they came across it if they were not in immediate danger of being caught.

For the most part, however, the pickings of the day, bits of food, remnants of clothing, and odds and ends of all types, were invariably brought back to the shelter in the Blind to be shared among the group. Any item thought to be of any value was brought to a man at the far end of the Blind who might pay them a penny or two for it.

Bates, age twelve, was the undisputed leader of the group even though he was a year younger than Tom, whose surname the others never knew, as indeed perhaps neither did Tom himself. Bates was a natural leader and no one else in the band ever openly challenged his authority. He used his innate organizational skills to plan frequent forays into other sections of Dublin or to delegate duties and assignments to the other boys. He was much taller than any of the others, had both the mental and physical toughness to do whatever survival demanded of him, and ruled the little band with a fierce passion. It was his kingdom.

Bates also possessed another quality – the natural basic instincts of a parent. Wherever the band went, he always kept Lame Harry in his view because he knew that the boy's withered leg would make it difficult for him to keep up with the others or to flee at the first sign of danger. Sometimes at night, when Jimmy, the youngest, woke up sobbing, as he did on many nights, Bates would cradle him in his arms and croon softly to him or tell him stories while the other boys slept.

Thus, the sad little band of homeless boys managed to keep themselves alive on the streets of Dublin. There was little other option. For to them, life on the street was infinitely better than an existence in any of the crammed orphanages of the city. Their aversion to orphanage life was reinforced by the horrific tales told to them by Tom, who had once lived in such an institution before running away. Even less desirable was the alternative of working in any of the city's vast, gray tinder-box factories that made immense profits for their wealthy owners on the cheap labour provided by countless thousands of homeless and destitute children.

The blond-haired boy with the strange blue eyes fitted in well from the beginning. He spoke very little. Only Fat Harry, whose short body was almost obese despite the pitifully scant amount of food that passed through his lips each day and who seldom spoke except in guttural grunts, talked less. Despite his quiet ways, the blond boy was efficient, a keen observer and a quick learner, and he rapidly became very adept at his work. Within a year he had so perfected the art of his craft that his expertise greatly enhanced the overall quality of food, clothing, and other necessities of life for the entire band.

He had by this time also grown into a particularly close relationship with Bates, and he and Bates often undertook excursions of their own further and further afield while the others waited in the Blind for their return.

As they grew older, he and Bates became bolder and more daring in their endeavors. The nature of their activities gradually escalated beyond the mere scrummaging around for bits of food and clothing to keep their bodies and souls intact. They now routinely engaged in pickpocketing, purse snatching, and were not even averse to burglary whenever an opportunity presented itself. They found the pickings south of the River Liffey, which flowed through the city dividing it in half, to be the best of all. There, particularly in the areas around St. Patrick's and Christ Church Cathedrals and Dublin Castle, hordes of people constantly moved in crowded proximity, ripe and easy targets for the boys' deft fingers. While they still returned to the shelter in the Blind each night, they grew increasingly apart from the others. They now took their stolen items, some of which at times were of significant value, to a fence in another part of the city whom they had learned about from some other boys of the street.

The fence, oddly, was a woman known as Nanny Williams. Her age was indeterminable. Short and thin, her inscrutable face, with its myriad lines and wrinkles and small black eyes set far back in their sockets, hid her secrets well. A tiny cruel mouth that appeared to have been clamped shut by nature disguised the absence of all but a few misshapen and decayed teeth. She might have been forty. She might have been seventy. No one knew for sure.

Nanny Williams had taken an immediate liking to the blond, blue-eyed boy who always seemed content to let Bates do all the talking, and for a brief period of about six weeks, when he was fifteen, he had enjoyed the luxury of sleeping under her

roof each night. He did not sleep in a bed or in a room, but just inside the door in the darkness of a narrow hall that led to the other rooms of the house, none of which he had ever seen. It was, however, warmer, safer and more comfortable than the shelter in the Blind. Bates, to whom she had taken an instant dislike for some unknown reason, was never invited inside.

Although it was obvious to both boys that Nanny Williams' business operations extended somewhere beyond fencing, they could never figure out what it fully encompassed. Even though she often employed them to run errands for her, neither of the boys had ever summoned up enough nerve to give in to the temptation to open any of the small packages that they had been given to deliver, and the messages that she sometimes asked them to relay were so strange and garbled that they made no sense at all to them.

One day, as the two boys were running such an errand, Bates confided out of the blue that, "Nanny Williams is a witch, you know." He said he had heard it from some of the other street boys who worked the same area.

That same night, when the blond boy returned to the house, Nanny caught him looking at her with such intensity and for so long that she was finally moved to ask him, "What are ye looking at, boy? Ye better not be up to any devilment with me or you'll soon rue the day you set eyes on me, you little beggar."

Before he knew what he was doing, the boy blurted out, "Bates says you're a witch. And that you can see things, even the future."

The woman froze where she stood as if struck. The look that she gave him chilled him to the bone. He suddenly felt very afraid. Unable to meet her gaze, he looked away. Then, with a loud cackle, the woman laughed, "Maybe I can. And maybe I can't."

The spell broken, the boy seized the moment and somehow summoned up enough nerve to bring his eyes back to her lined face, and stammered, "Will you tell me my future?"

For several more moments neither the woman nor the boy spoke or moved. They stared into each others eyes. This time, however, the boy did not falter or drop his gaze. Finally, with what seemed to the boy to be a long sigh, Nanny reached forward to take his sweating hand into her own long bony fingers, looked deep into his mind and soul, and told him what she saw. That night the boy hardly slept at all as the things that the woman had told him tumbled over and over in his mind until morning broke and he was back on the street.

Three days later, as he was making his way back to Nanny's house at the end of another day on the streets, he was intercepted by Bates, who breathlessly told him not to go in. Hours earlier the police had come and taken Nanny Williams away. That night the blond boy returned to the shelter in the Blind. Neither he nor Bates ever saw Nanny Williams again, and they never did discover the full scope and true nature of Nanny's business operations.

The tiny band of boys stayed together for a period of seven years, held together by the common bond of hunger and the fear of being alone in the world. Somewhere along the way two other boys had made their way into the group, and they all grew older together. Some of them were by this time almost grown men. They still retained possession of the shelter in the Blind. Several months earlier they had repulsed a second attempt by another band of boys to oust them, but had prevailed in the defense of their home and were now older and big enough to defend it from all comers.

Thanks mainly to the more adventurous endeavors of Bates and the blond boy, they were much better off than they had been in the earlier years. In that entire period, not a single one of them had ever been caught in any of their crimes, none of them had ever experienced any serious illness despite the filthy conditions under which they existed, and they had all continued to get along well with each other. They had lived a charmed life.

And then their luck ran out – especially for Bates and the blond boy.

For several days the two boys had been watching the premises of Callahan, the watchmaker. They knew that the old man lived alone in rooms above the small shop that he owned and, from all appearances, operated by himself. They knew to the minute when he would draw the iron grill across his storefront door before closing for the day. They knew when he took his evening meal, and when he retired for the night. They knew his full routine by heart. And they had devised a plan to relieve him of some of his valuables.

Not many nights later, under the cover of darkness and one of the heavy, dense, yellow fogs that descend upon the city of Dublin several times a year, ideal conditions for their undertaking, they made their move. Their plan was a simple one. It depended on swiftness of execution, a fast exit, and a bit of luck in the gamble that nobody would venture past in the lateness of the hour while they were at their work. They planned to simply break the glass of the small window in the front of the shop, enter, and in the space of a minute or two at most, cram as much as they could get their hands on into the gunny sack that they would bring with them and into their pockets, and then make their escape into the darkness of the city. They judged that the public gaslight located directly in front of the old man's shop would, despite the fog, provide them with just enough light to see what they were doing inside.

But even the simplest and best made plans sometimes fail. The two boys had scarcely begun to gather up their booty when their actions were suddenly interrupted by loud and angry shouting from above. There, at the top of the stairs, was the old man, awakened by the sound of the breaking glass, raining down threats and curses on them. Even though this possibility had previously occurred to them, the boys were momentarily frozen into immobility by his sudden appearance. Nevertheless they quickly tried to cram a few more valuables into their bag before making their exit through the broken window.

In the faint light that filtered into the store from the gaslight outside, however, they saw the old man suddenly totter at the top of the staircase. They watched in horror as he fell and tumbled down the stairs. His head seemed to strike every step as he descended until he finally landed in a crumpled heap at the bottom of the stairs. The grotesque angle at which his neck stood off from the rest of his body told the boys that the old man was dead and clearly beyond help of any kind.

Bates had the presence of mind to immediately flee into the night. The blond boy, however, made no attempt to move. Indeed, he couldn't. He was so paralyzed by the sight of the old man's broken body at the bottom of the stairs and the wide open sightless eyes that still stared accusingly at him, that his blood ran cold in his veins and he felt sick to his stomach.

Shocked beyond comprehension, he was scarcely aware of the presence of the two policemen who had come to take him away. He had no way of knowing that Bates had also been taken only minutes after bolting through the broken window.

The nightmare succession of events of the ensuing few days culminated in him standing in chains and leg irons before the judge who only minutes earlier had sentenced Bates to be hanged for his part in the robbery and death of the old man. Bates had just turned eighteen.

The blond boy, now in the seventh month of his sixteenth year, expected no less. However, something in the boy, whether it was the unwavering gaze of his clear blue eyes or the forthright manner in which he had told his story, struck a chord somewhere within the tired old judge who had seen the dregs of humanity dragged before his court every day for more years than he cared to recount, and he had shown a shred of compassion for the boy. Instead of hanging him, like Bates, he sentenced him to a life of hard labour in prison, to be served in the infamous Queenshythe Prison in England.

four

When the iron gates of Queenshythe Prison clanged shut behind him, the blond boy was devoid of all feeling. The events of the preceding days had so numbed his body and soul that he was virtually stripped of the capacity to feel emotion of any kind.

The inside of Queenshythe, like many of the other prisons in England, comprised a number of blocks, or compounds, where as many as forty or fifty prisoners might share a single large, open space and serve their prison sentences together in crammed intimacy. The few individual cells that the prison had were reserved for prisoners of extreme importance or those who had committed some crime so heinous or so sensational that there was no choice but to isolate them from the other prisoners. The government of the day had neither the inclination nor the financial wherewithal to provide individual accommodations for all.

However, in an attempt to bring some semblance of order to the chaotic conditions of the jails, the authorities who ran the country's penal system tried to group the prisoners into criminals, like petty thieves and those imprisoned for indebtedness, with each other. Sometimes mistakes were made and the intended groupings were not strictly adhered to. Nobody, however, cared a great deal when this occurred except perhaps the unfortunate man or woman who happened to be placed in some compound whose inmates were more violent and dangerous than his or her own crime warranted.

Every prison compound, regardless of its classification, was a dangerous and violent place. Even the prison's guards and wardens rarely ventured into the open areas. Food and water for the prisoners were simply passed in for the inmates to distribute among themselves, which often resulted in a chaotic situation that left some of the prisoners without their fair share and others with double portions. Inmates emptied their bladders and bowels into pails or into small grill-covered holes in the floor that were connected to a complex underground sewer system that eventually flowed into the nearby River Thames. The overpowering stench of human waste, unwashed bodies and stagnant air permeated the area without cessation.

Under this arrangement, it was difficult for the prison administrators to effectively control the violence that always took place within the compounds. Indeed, on many occasions they simply turned a blind eye to whatever was happening inside. Invariably, in every compound, some form of hierarchical structure would develop, in which a handful of the strongest and cruelest inmates ruled, making life for those at the bottom of the order a virtual living hell. The blond boy, because of the nature of his sentence, was placed with the murderers.

His indoctrination into life in Queenshythe Prison, one of the vilest in the entire penal system of England, would be swift and immediate. Only hours after his arrival as he stood alone trying to take in his new surroundings, still dazed, he found himself surrounded by three men, all of whom had suddenly materialized with obvious intent to accost him in some manner.

"Well now, pretty boy, what have we here?" The malevolent toothless grin of the man addressing him bespoke the evil that resided within him. The other two men pressed closer. The boy instinctively shrank away, but his every movement was effectively blocked by the others. Other nearby prisoners, whether they were aware of what was about to take place or not, kept their distance. The boy was left to his own devices. He felt a fear in the pit of his stomach worse than anything he had ever known in his seven years on the streets of Dublin.

The man who had spoken was the obvious leader of the three men. When he reached forward and tilted the boy's head back to study his soft youthful, yet-to-be-shaved face, the normal din of the compound died away to a hushed silence. Most of the other prisoners, now aware of what was happening, looked on, some in gleeful anticipation of what they were about to witness, others with revulsion, some with compassion for the boy.

"Now, blue eyes. Welcome to hell. Nothing can help you now. You're ours."

The stark fear that paralyzed the boy showed plainly on his face as his tormentor laughed softly, his sinister countenance betraying the sadistic pleasure that he was obviously taking from the moment.

Further movement of the man, however, was suddenly arrested by two massive hands that clamped his neck and shoulders in a vice grip from which he had no chance of escape, no matter how hard he might struggle and squirm. Neither of the other two men made any move to help him.

"Lay a finger on him and ye'll answer to me."

The man who had come to the new boy's rescue towered over every other man in the compound. His massive head and shoulders, the bulk of his rock-iron frame, and the belligerent glare that he cast about him, dared any and all to come at him. Finally he relinquished his grip on the other man, defusing the tense situation and with no further comment quietly led the boy away to the far corner of the compound.

"There now, lad, they'll not bother you again if you stay close to me."

The man was Ned Finn, serving a life sentence for strangling another man with his bare hands several years earlier, and he would, from that moment, become the boy's protector, asking nothing in return, content to see that the blond, blue-eyed youth came to no harm in his evil and violent surroundings.

Queenshythe Prison was not a place where prisoners were permitted to stand around idly for much of their time. Most of its inmates had been sent there to serve their sentences at hard labor. Deep within the center of the prison complex, whose many blocks and compounds sprawled over several acres of land, was the rock yard. The complex system of blocks and tackles that hoisted the huge granite boulders into the work area every day was an engineering marvel of its time. There, with rock mauls, sledgehammers, axes, saws and other implements, the prisoners, under the scrutiny of an army of armed guards numbering almost as many as the inmates themselves, transformed the huge rocks into smaller rectangles of stone measuring about two feet by four feet and a foot-and-a-half in depth. This output of the unlimited supply of free labor provided by the prisons of England was used throughout the city of London and elsewhere in the country for the construction of government buildings, courthouses, churches, bridges and other public structures of all kinds. It was backbreaking toil that eventually broke the bodies and spirits of most of the men who performed it.

The blond boy languished in Queenshythe prison for eight years, during which time he grew into full manhood. For the first two years, he survived solely under the protection of Ned Finn. While the three men who had initially accosted him sometimes still threatened and menaced him from a distance, they never ventured close enough to do either him or Finn, or themselves, any real harm.

The swill that passed for food for the inmates left most of them greatly undernourished, thin, and constantly hungry. The body of the blond boy, however, seemed to find everything that it needed in the poor fare, and he thrived and grew strong and healthy on it. The work in the rock yard that bent and twisted other men also seemed to agree with him. His arms, shoulders, chest, legs, and the muscles of his now rock-hard body continued to develop and he gradually grew into a well-proportioned muscular specimen of manhood.

He was now quite capable of holding his own in any situation that arose within the compound and no longer needed the protection of Finn. Still, he and Finn maintained their friendship and continued to provide mutual protection and companionship for each other as the months and years slowly passed.

Having gotten past his first few months in the hell hole of Queenshythe Prison, during which his mind and soul had plummeted to the deepest depths of despair, he finally reconciled himself to his life of confinement and labour. Somewhere deep within him, however, he held fast to the belief that someday some miracle would occur and he would be free again. More than anything else, his undying hope for freedom was rooted in the words that Nanny Williams had told him that night many years earlier.

"You poor pitiful wretch. There's not much of anything good I can tell you, boy, for you were born a child of misfortune and

bad luck. And it's not over yet, for I see many more years of misery and suffering ahead for you. I see you standing in a strange faraway land. I see great sadness and distress. But in the end, before you die, I see freedom and contentment, and even happiness. You'll live a hard life. But I promise you that you will die a happy man."

And, in the eighth year of his imprisonment, the miracle that he had hoped for and believed in materialized. The jails of England had become so crowded that, no matter how densely the prisoners were packed in, the prisons could no longer accommodate the hundreds of newly convicted criminals that passed through the courts of England every day. King George II and his government, faced with the prospect of having to dip into an already depleted treasury to build more jails, instead searched for other alternatives.

Throughout England, hundreds of prisoners originally sentenced to be hanged but whose executions had thus far been deferred or delayed, now met their deaths in quick order on hastily constructed gallows all across the country. Shiploads of others convicted of lesser offences were transported to serve out their sentences in the penal colonies of Australia, and hundreds of others were transported to Newfoundland and America where they would live a life of bondage and servitude in the colonies that England had established in these lands.

A much smaller number, the ablest and the fittest, were told that they were to serve for the rest of their lives, until they were no longer fit for the work, in His Majesty's Royal Navy. They were promised that at the end they would be left to spend their remaining days somewhere in anonymity and freedom. Although preferable to a continued life of imprisonment for most, it was nevertheless another yet more subtle form of involuntary recruitment and many of them would quickly find out that life in His Majesty's Royal Navy for men like them would be every bit as cruel and brutal as their time in prison. The policy of clearing out the country's prisons in this manner gave the navy a welcomed chance to replenish their ranks without having to resort to their usual press-gang tactics. Normally, gangs of thugs, armed with truncheons and the

"King's shilling,"[1] roamed the cities and the countryside doing the navy's dirty work by taking unsuspecting prospects by trickery or force and delivering them, usually drunk or unconscious, to warships and other naval vessels ready to put to sea. For many of the conscripts thus recruited, their first inkling of what had happened to them came upon awakening hundreds of miles from shore.

Still, the blond boy, now a man, unlike many of the others, had immediately welcomed the opportunity. The chance for a new life outside the penal environment was what had dominated his thoughts every day from the moment he first entered Queenshythe Prison eight years earlier. He had resolved himself to do everything within his power to ensure that he would never be sent back there, or to any prison anywhere.

But now, lying in pain and despair in the darkness of the infirmary, he knew that by trying to come to Ned Finn's rescue he had wasted his only chance for freedom, and feared that the rest of his life would surely now be spent in confinement. Little did he realize as he lay there, his blond hair and beard matted with his own blood and vomit, and the festering scars on his shredded back emitting their own putrid odor, that his name would one day ring down through the annals of Newfoundland, the large island on the other side of the Atlantic to which he was now surely destined to be transported.

He was Peter Kerrivan, and his name would live on in the hearts of countless future generations of Newfoundlanders as a symbol of defiance, freedom, perseverance, and endurance.

---

[1] The standard "contract of commitment" upon entering the navy was one shilling. In many cases, the shilling was hidden in the bottom of a mug of ale or rum by a member of the press-gang and the unsuspecting prospect, by virtue of consuming the free drink, in effect accepted the shilling and hence recruitment into the navy.

five

The Italian explorer, Giovanni Caboto, had made his famous voyage to Newfoundland two hundred and fifty-three years earlier. Known as John Cabot to future generations of Newfoundlanders, he was a bold and persistent man. When his proposed voyage to the west to try to find a new and hopefully shorter route to Cathay was rejected by Spain, and in turn by Portugal, he had prevailed in his search for a sponsor when he finally found enough interest in his proposed endeavor in England to convince that country to underwrite the cost of his venture into the vast unknown. Or, more specifically, the merchants of Bristol, who were probably as interested, perhaps even more so, in the possibility of finding new fishing grounds as they were in the discovery of any new route to the Orient.

Cabot failed in his attempt to discover the new route that he was looking for despite the fact that he had sailed further westward than any man before him. His voyage itself, however, wasn't a failure for what he did find was of infinitely more value to England than any alternate route to Cathay would ever prove to be. Upon returning to England, he told his sponsors that the waters surrounding the large island that he had discovered two thousand miles away teemed with codfish so plentiful that they could be dipped up from the ocean in baskets without the use of nets of any kind. He called the island the New Founde Land, and the merchants of Bristol knew then that they had struck gold. From that date onward for the next hundred years or more, England, followed in rapid succession by France, Spain and Portugal, would send a steady stream of ships westward each spring and summer to reap the bountiful harvest of the New Founde Land's coastal waters to help feed their burgeoning populations. Their ships returned filled to their full capacities without fail year after year, and the merchants of Bristol and London, and their counterparts in the other countries, grew incredibly wealthy.

The New Founde Land, which would be shortened to simply Newfoundland with the passage of time, offered many other valuables besides fish. The vast tracts of timberland and forests of the large 43,000 square mile island, as well as its great inland rivers and lakes, mineral deposits, wildlife, great seal herds, and its myriad other natural resources, even some arable farmland, were there for the taking. But the fishing merchants of Bristol and London and elsewhere, even if they recognized Newfoundland's full potential, showed little interest in anything other than the commodity that continued to fill their coffers to overflowing. Indeed, in conspiratorial agreement with France and the other European countries, they went to great lengths to protect their investment in Newfoundland by doing everything within their power to prohibit any permanent settlement there. They had quickly come to the realization that their vested interests could best be served by maintaining Newfoundland as a large seasonal fishing station.

In the years immediately following Cabot's voyage of discovery, a number of temporary fishing stations were established along the coastline of Newfoundland. Names like Fermeuse, Reneuse (Renews), Aquaforte, Placentia and Spaniard's Bay attest to the presence of the French, Spanish and Portuguese in Newfoundland, in addition to the English, as early as the beginning of the sixteenth century.

The policy of anti-colonization begun by the Bristol and London merchants would remain in effect for more than a hundred years. Although a handful of men were sometimes purposely left to over-winter in Newfoundland, they were not considered colonists. They were simply left there temporarily to do some work in preparation for the following year or to protect their fishing station from the ravages of the other countries who often raided and pillaged their holdings.

Despite the ban against permanent settlement and the best efforts of the authorities, during this hundred-year time span dozens of tiny settlements sprang into surreptitious existence in many of the hidden coves and inlets of Newfoundland's coastline. There, a handful of men and a few women, hidden from the prying eyes of the frigates that constantly prowled the coast and other ships passing by, were willing to brave the cold winters of the island, and the wrath of the authorities if they were caught, to carve out an existence for themselves in this harsh island wilderness. Most of these tiny settlements and hamlets would disappear with the passage of time, but some would survive and centuries later become important contributors to the fishing economy on which Newfoundland would continue to base its survival.

Then, in the early 1600's, the attitude in England toward the settlement of Newfoundland began to slowly change when a group of more farsighted merchants, including John Guy, himself a Bristol merchant, advocated the establishment of a permanent colony. They were successful in convincing others of the potential value of such an initiative. In 1610, a small group of thirty-nine colonists set out from Bristol led by Guy himself, sailed westward, and established the first official colony in Newfoundland. They chose as their site Cuper's Cove (later called Cupids) in Conception Bay, so-named by the Portuguese a century earlier in honor of the Feast of the Conception.

By all accounts, the settlement of Cupids was a successful venture, thanks in large part to an abnormally mild first winter which was virtually free of storms and frost. This permitted the colonists to lay the foundation of Newfoundland's first permanent settlement and erect the various structures that it would need. Although Guy himself returned to England after only three years in Newfoundland, the tiny foothold that he left behind survived and would pave the way for others to follow. Ironically, it is believed that upon his return to England, Guy, for reasons unclear, fell into disagreement with the other merchants who had participated with him in the venture and spent his remaining years disenchanted with the policy of colonization that he had ushered into being.

Buoyed by the success of Cupids and the relative ease with which the first colony in Newfoundland had been established, the swing in England toward further colonization of Newfoundland (and America), gained momentum and a scant eleven years later the second permanent settlement in

五

Newfoundland, the Colony of Avalon, was established on the site of the seasonal fishing station known as Ferryland.

George Calvert (later to be knighted and known as Lord Baltimore for his long years of meritorious service in the British Parliament and personal assistance to the King) volunteered to lead the new undertaking across the Atlantic. He was Secretary of State for England at the time and had been successful in acquiring a tract of land in Newfoundland that ranged from a point of land somewhere between the fishing stations of Fermeuse and Aquaforte north about five miles to Caplin Bay. Not long after, before he himself departed for Newfoundland for the first time, he was successful in obtaining a charter for a much larger tract of territory that encompassed most of the entire large peninsula that he would later call the Peninsula of Avalon.

Calvert and his family, and a group of about forty additional settlers, all of whom were Roman Catholic, arrived in Ferryland in the summer of 1628. Their attraction to the newly founded settlement was short-lived. Calvert's family, especially his wife, did not have the hardiness or the staying power of the hundred or more men and women whom he had sent ahead of him, some as early as 1621, to prepare the colony. After a single winter in the Colony of Avalon, during which their food supply ran out, severe storms blew almost without cessation and temperatures fell to abysmal lows, and the settlement was subjected to raids and harassment by pirates and marauding French sailors, Calvert and his entourage returned to England. He did, however, maintain his interest in the colonization program and at his request was granted a tract of land to establish another colony in the warmer climate of Maryland in America.[2]

Historians are divided in their opinion of Calvert's motivation for volunteering to spearhead the effort to establish the Colony of Avalon. Some believe that he did it out of duty to his king and country. Others argue that he wanted to create a safe haven for Roman Catholics who were still being persecuted in England at that time. Still others contend that he did it simply

[2] The colony of Maryland was actually established by his son, Lord Baltimore II, after Calvert's death.

for personal financial gain.

Whatever his motive, the Colony of Avalon, like Cupids, survived in the absence of the man who had created it, and would in the fullness of time achieve and maintain a position of significance and importance in Newfoundland history, both from a historical and economic perspective. It was also the beginning of the dominant Roman Catholic presence that has prevailed along the length and breadth of the Southern Shore of the Avalon Peninsula to this day.

Continuing a custom begun early in the sixteenth century, law and order in the Colony of Avalon, as elsewhere in Newfoundland, was administered by an ill-conceived arrangement known as the Fishing Admirals System. In the absence of a permanent year-round Governor or law enforcement official of any kind, the master of the first ship to enter the harbor in the spring of the year was recognized as the Admiral of the Colony for the remainder of the fishing season. The second and third fishing masters to arrive were his assistants, the Vice-Admiral and the Rear-Admiral, and together they were responsible for the enforcement of justice in the area for that year. This informal arrangement was repeated in many other harbors along Newfoundland's hundreds of miles of coastline.

Needless to say, the quality of justice under the Fishing Admirals System was questionable at best, nor was it standardized or consistent. The Admirals, rough and ready men themselves, were more often than not poorly educated or even illiterate. It is doubtful whether many of them, whose main purpose in Newfoundland was to make a profitable fishing voyage, dedicated much of their time to dispensing law and order in a fair and proper manner. In most cases those accused of serious crimes were simply packed off to England to be dealt with there, while lesser offences often went unresolved and disputes left unsettled. The Admirals also undoubtedly took advantage of their positions of privilege to make judgements suitable to their own interests and to choose the best fishing rooms for themselves and their friends.

Still, despite its many shortcomings, the Fishing Admirals System remained in effect for more than two hundred years. Finally, in 1729, the constant pressure of complaints from residents of the Island and other fishing masters convinced the British Government of the inadequacy of the system and they appointed the first of a succession of Naval Governors in the person of Sir Henry Osborne. Even then it would be many more years before a proper system of courts and magistrates was fully implemented. The Fishing Admiral System was never formally abolished or legislated out of existence, but simply died out with the introduction of properly appointed year-round law officials.

Many of the men and women in the Colony of Avalon and the other colonies and settlements of Newfoundland during this period were indentured to the fishing masters and planters who had brought them over from England and Ireland as laborers. Some of them, mainly young Irishmen and boys, had actually been purchased in Ireland for the going price of fifty pounds and lived in virtual slavery to the masters who owned them. With rare exception, they were cruelly treated, ill-clothed, poorly fed, and valued only for the raw labour that they performed. Sometimes they were required to work as much as fifteen or twenty hours a day. Although the laws of Newfoundland at the time decreed that they had to be paid for their labour, usually ten pounds a year, very few of them ever received anywhere close to that amount or were able to save enough to buy out the indentureship, and hence their freedom, once all deductions had been made from their wages and all credits against them settled up.

During this same period, thousands of others, many of whom had run away from their masters, squatted on land owned by the Crown or set up residence in small coves and inlets along the coast, where they fished using crudely built shallops, and sold their catches to the larger fishing merchants. They were a thorn in the side of the merchants who much preferred the cheaper and more profitable system of indentured labor, but their existence, while frowned upon, was for the most part tolerated and ignored. And they, more than anyone else, would be the people who would eventually settle the full length and breadth of the Island and shape the culture and character that would make Newfoundland unique in the world.

SIX

O n May 29th, 1750, the twenty-third year of King George II's reign of England and Scotland, the *Fortress* made its appearance in the Colony of Avalon. No one had any inkling of its coming until the large frigate was suddenly dropping anchor in the middle of the harbor, looming like a ghostly apparition in the fog and mist.

The colony had by this time reverted to its original name of Ferryland or more specifically in the language of the time, as the Plantation of Ferryland, although the only crops grown there were vegetables to feed its people, a few herbs, and perhaps a sprinkling of flowers to brighten their days. On the day that the *Fortress* came, a massive bank of dense, low-lying fog blanketed the Southern Shore from Petty Harbour in the north to Trepassey, almost a hundred miles to the south. The cold, penetrating drizzle that had been falling intermittently for two days had dampened and soaked everything outside, prompting the people of the dozen or more small settlements that dotted the Southern Shore to look for chores and tasks that would keep them indoors as much as possible.

Despite the uncomfortable weather, the entire population of the colony converged on the point of beach where the delegation that was being rowed ashore would touch land. Anxious for news and information from England, they welcomed the diversion from their usual mundane chores and dropped everything else that they had been doing at the time. There the delegation was met by Lieutenant Stanford, commanding officer of the Ferryland garrison and the presiding authority of the settlement. When Captain Smith and his entourage of senior officers were escorted by Stanford to the garrison headquarters, the residents turned their attention to the sailors who had rowed them ashore, still thirsty for even the tiniest tidbit of news from the country that many of them still thought of as home.

Inside the garrison, when the courtesies and the protocols had been properly observed, the discussion turned to the more pressing business at hand. As was the custom when representatives of the crown or senior naval officers like Smith visited, Lieutenant Stanford provided a detailed report on the status of the Ferryland Plantation, outlining the events of the preceding months and the plans and expectations for the coming year knowing that Captain Smith, upon his eventual return to England, would file the report with his superiors. Stanford also knew that Smith's report would be used to validate what he himself had already submitted in his own earlier dispatches.

Next came the matter of fresh water and food to replenish the *Fortress's* dwindling supplies. And, finally, after that, the disposition of some of the prisoners that the *Fortress* was carrying, that being the primary purpose of the ship's voyage, firstly to Newfoundland and subsequently to America.

Stanford, always eager to take advantage of any free labor that would enable him to carry out some of the repairs that the perennially under-manned garrison constantly needed and to undertake some of the other projects that he had been envisioning for some time, agreed to take eight of the men. He would have gladly taken more, but the garrison did not have the armed capacity to effectively guard and supervise more than that number and still be able to keep the large group of indentured men and women that he already had working there in check.

Lieutenant Stanford was an ambitious but hard and sometimes brutal man. He had languished in Ferryland for more years than he wished to recall, knowing that the longer he was left there, the more likely he was to be forgotten and overlooked by his superiors in England while his naval career lapsed into anonymity. Although he was only a lieutenant, he had been in charge of the garrison and responsible for law and order in the area since Naval Governor Curtis had become terminally ill four years ago and gone back to England. No one had yet been sent to replace him, leaving Stanford in a position of responsibility way above his rank. He had experienced a slight flicker of hope that his recall to England may have been at hand when the *Fortress* suddenly appeared in the harbor. He had dismissed the thought in almost the same instant, however, for he had been disappointed and let down too many times before.

Trapped in circumstances beyond his control, short of resigning his position altogether or deserting, he often took out his frustrations on his own officers and the indentured men and women of the Plantation. He had the responsibility to see that they were properly fed and cared for as directed by the naval regulations that he had to observe, but he otherwise showed little or no feeling toward them.

Stanford, despite his disillusionment and sometimes violent nature, nevertheless knew how to be a good host. That night, when all the business matters had been concluded, he treated his guests, Captain Smith and his officers, to a fine supper of roasted hen, baked codfish, boiled potatoes, and greens, followed by a cream custard and a choice of pies, all washed down with a generous supply of good red wine that materialized whenever anyone's glass neared empty. Afterward, the visitors all took port or sherry in another room of the garrison, luxuriating in the comfort of their first evening on shore in almost a month. It was nearly midnight when they were finally rowed back to the ship.

Despite the lateness of the hour, Captain Smith was anxious to make preparations for the delivery of the eight promised men at the first light of day. At his direction, the selected men were assembled on the quarterdeck where they would spend the next few hours before being brought ashore and turned over to the garrison. They were protected from the rain and drizzle by a large piece of canvas stretched over the deck. Among the first to be chosen were Kerrivan, Finn, and Styles. Having made his preparations, Smith retired for the night, pleased with himself to be rid of the three troublesome men so easily.

He had no way of knowing at the time, after such an enjoyable evening on shore and perhaps still basking in the bonhomie of the occasion, if not the many glasses of wine and port he had consumed, that he had just made a fatal error in judgement – one that would be the only blight on an otherwise admirable and distinguished career, and one that would haunt him for the rest of his life.

At daybreak, eight men were delivered as promised to

Lieutenant Stanford in the garrison. They did not, however, include Kerrivan, Finn or Styles. Astonishingly, the three men had escaped, disappearing as if by magic sometime in the darkness of the early morning hours.

Captain Smith, as furious with himself as he was with the officers and men who had somehow permitted this unspeakable event to occur, demanded that Stanford, despite the earliness of the hour, assemble the residents of the Plantation to find out if anyone had seen the escaped men or had any knowledge of their whereabouts.

When the large bell that had been used for a hundred years or more to sound the alarm whenever enemy ships approached was rung, the men and women of the Plantation quickly dressed and made their way to the garrison. There, in the cold drizzle that continued to saturate everything in the Plantation, Captain Smith told the residents about the escape of the three men and asked for their help and cooperation in recapturing them.

After a suitable period of waiting in which no response was forthcoming, Smith, still smarting, reminded the settlers of the personal risk to anyone who might have in any way aided or abetted the three men in their flight. Before returning to his ship in the harbor, Smith had his officers post a notice in the center of the Plantation, making it clear that anyone found helping the fugitives or withholding information that could possibly lead to their recapture, would experience the full wrath of British law.

The following day, the *Fortress* sailed into the harbors of Aquaforte and Fermeuse, and the day after that into Renews and Cappahayden, where the entire populations of these settlements were assembled and addressed by Captain Smith in a similar manner. At no time in any of these settlements did anyone come forward with any information of a meaningful nature.

Indeed, in all truth, they couldn't – for no one in Ferryland, Aquaforte, Fermeuse, Renews or Cappahayden, not a single man, woman, or child had seen or heard the three men in their flight. They had simply vanished.

seven

The small mountain known as the Butterpot, at nine hundred and fifty feet above sea level, is the highest point of land on the Southern Shore of the Avalon Peninsula. Lying inland about five miles due west of the settlement of Fermeuse, it was still as pristine and unsullied by man in the days of the Ferryland Plantation as it had been when the large peninsula on which it is situated had first risen from the sea. No trodden footpaths, charred campfire remains or any other markings of man gave any evidence that anyone had ever walked there. Only if a person searched around long enough and hard enough might he eventually find the smooth remains of some sawn tree trunk to suggest that some solitary soul had at one time been successful in his search for a bent spruce knee suitable for a shallop's prow. The rare free spirit who may have at one time climbed to the top of the mountain, which in reality was not much more than a large hill, just for the view, left no lasting evidence of his presence there at all.

And what a magnificent view it was. To the east the mountain afforded an unobstructed view of some of the small fishing settlements that dotted the nearby twelve-mile section of coastline and beyond that, as far as the eye could see, the vast unbroken expanse of ocean that stretched eastward for more than two thousand miles.

The Butterpot was strewn with huge rocks and boulders deposited there by the gigantic glaciers that had moved over the peninsula millions of years earlier. The sparse scattering of spruce that grew on the eastern slope of the mountain was, despite its ancient years, small, stunted, and twisted by the prevailing southeasterly winds that had blown in from the Atlantic unchecked and unhindered from the beginning of time. Most of the land that lay between the mountain and the sea, except for the thin ribbon of forest that paralleled the coast, was barren, covered by gorse, dwarf ground spruce, caribou moss, and the purplish-green ground cover that the people of the area had come to call goudie or goowithy, and here and there small pockets of alders, spruce, fir and juniper trees. Dozens of small ponds and bog-holes dotted the area, and berries of many types, including blueberries, partridgeberries, bakeapples, raspberries, wild cherries and wild plums, grew there in abundance. Hares, foxes, partridge and other forms of small wildlife inhabited the region, although larger animals, with the exception of caribou, were rarely known to have frequented the area in any significant numbers.

Of the dozens of small streams and rivulets that sprang from underground springs on the slope of the mountain and around its base, only one ever eventually made it all the way to the sea. In its quest for freedom, this tiny stream inched its way over the gradual southeast slope of the land to merge with another small trickle like itself which flowed from a pond about halfway to the coast, and beyond that point joins numerous other small brooks and streams to finally form the river known as Peter's Brook that emptied into Renews Harbour, about seven miles distant from the mountain where the tiny stream had first sprung forth.

The other little rivulets of fresh water that started out from the mountain, most of them mere trickles, all died along the way either by being absorbed into the numerous landlocked ponds and bog holes that barred their way, or by simply disappearing into the ground.

The view from the other side of the Butterpot mountain, while still spectacular, was not quite as varied. Only open barrens, lakes, ponds, and occasional patches of forest covered the large tract of land that stretched westward for more than thirty miles to St. Mary's Bay on the other side of the Avalon Peninsula.

The early morning sky was clear. The cold rain and drizzle that had fallen steadily during the days preceding and following the arrival of the *Fortress* in Ferryland Harbour had finally ceased. A fresh westerly wind had dissipated the fog in all but a few of the lower lying valleys and wales. In the faint light of the false dawn a few stars still glittered overhead although the moon had already run its full course and was no longer visible in the sky. The silence of the mountain was broken only by the conversation of a few enterprising early rising birds and the gentle sighing of the wind in the trees. The sounds of the sea and the early morning noises of the awakening settlements on the coast were lost in the distance.

In the stillness of the morning, there was nobody there, save the birds and the animals and the mountain itself, to witness the arrival of the three prisoners who had made their escape from the *Fortress* three days earlier. Within minutes of their coming, without having made any effort at all to inspect their new surroundings, the men were asleep, sprawled in the goowithy at the base of the mountain, no longer able or willing to stave off the fatigue and exhaustion that sapped the strength of their bodies and deadened their senses.

eight

I t was the first time since they had slipped over the side of the *Fortress*, more than forty-eight hours earlier, that Kerrivan, Finn, and Styles had been able to close their eyes for more than a few minutes at a time. So deep was their sleep already, having finally reached the sanctuary that they had been struggling toward for so long, that no dreams or images disturbed it. The tangle of events that had brought them from the ship to the mountain was completely forgotten for the moment.

When Captain Smith had assembled the eight prisoners for Lieutenant Stanford on the deck of the *Fortress* almost three days earlier, he had, without thinking clearly, made the mistake of leaving them in the custody of four men who, like himself, had been on shore all day in the Ferryland Plantation. He had, before retiring for the night, placed Ensign Sturge in charge, who, along with three able-bodied seamen from the ship's crew, assumed responsibility for the prisoners until they could be delivered ashore at dawn.

Kerrivan, Finn, Styles, and the other five prisoners that Smith had selected were confined to a small section of the deck where their four guardians could keep a close watch on them. They were individually manacled, but were not chained to the rail or linked together on a single long chain as prisoners sometimes were when they were brought on deck. They were even permitted to select their own resting places within the small designated area.

When they were told that the first man to attempt to move outside of this space would be shot without warning, they took it as no idle threat. For most of them, however, this was just another inconsequential occurrence in the overall treatment that they had long since come to expect as prisoners, and all they wanted to do now was to shield themselves as best they could from the night's cold air and get some sleep.

But not Kerrivan. Some primitive instinct kept him keenly alert and watchful while the others dozed off one by one. He was still awake at two o'clock in the morning when the first in a sequence of coincidental events occurred that would suddenly raise in him a small flicker of hope.

From his resting place near the rail, he heard the soft thump of some object as it butted gently against the side of the ship. Even before he looked, he knew what it was. It was undoubtedly one of the large logs that he had seen floating in the Ferryland Harbour earlier in the day when he had been brought on deck for his exercise period. They were the remnants of a much larger stack of logs that had been swept out into the harbor by an unusually high tide a few days earlier. Most of them had already been recovered, and only this one and a few others still remained at large. A quick glance over the side confirmed his assumption, for in the faint reflection of the running lanterns that had been left burning while the *Fortress* lay at anchor, he saw that the log lay alongside the ship almost directly below him.

A short while later, while the other prisoners slept, he was almost certain that Sturge and at least one, if not two of the seamen closest to him had also dozed off. He was right. Ensign Sturge, having been one of the guests wined and dined so lavishly by Lieutenant Stanford in the garrison only a few hours earlier, had consumed as much red wine and sherry as any man there although his appearance and actions didn't betray the fact. Now, in his blurred and fuzzy condition, he succumbed to the temptation to catch a few winks, abetted by the gentle rocking motion of the *Fortress* as she rode on her chains. His men would make sure that nothing happened.

What he didn't realize at the time was that the three other seamen had themselves, like him, also spent the day on shore. They had not returned to the *Fortress* after they had delivered Captain Smith and his entourage ashore, as Smith and his officers had assumed they would. The seamen would argue afterward that they had not been ordered to do so. They had instead spent the entire time with the citizens of the settlement, being wined and eight

dined themselves. The settlers, as they continued to grill the seamen for news and information from abroad, had fed them great
heaps of food and plied them with huge quantities of ale and rum.
And now, two of them, like Ensign Sturge, had, despite their best
efforts to stay awake, fallen asleep at their posts.

Every nerve of Kerrivan's body was as taut as a bowstring.
He instinctively knew in the pit of his stomach that he was
observing what was perhaps the only opportunity for escape
that he might ever have. He convinced himself that even if
he didn't succeed, he would be no worse off. Unless they shot
him – which they probably would because if he fled he would
then be, besides a convicted murderer, also a deserter from His
Majesty's Royal Navy.

Only one guard remained awake. Kerrivan reasoned that if
he could create some sort of diversion to attract the seaman's
attention elsewhere, he could be over the side in a flash and on
his way. He thought furiously about how he might bring such
an occurrence about. Then, even as he pondered his dilemma,
knowing that he didn't have very much time, he heard the
gentle snoring of that third seaman.

Placing his hand over the sleeping Ned Finn's mouth, he
nudged the big man awake. Finn, following the roll of
Kerrivan's eyes, immediately grasped the situation. Taking
great care to be as quiet as possible and to make no sudden
movements that might alert the others, Kerrivan stepped to
the rail and began to lower himself into the water where the log
awaited. Finn was only a step behind him.

Neither of them realized it at first, but a third man had also
followed right on their heels as they made their escape over the
side. Styles, the Snitch, had not been sleeping either, and had
taken in everything that was happening around him. When he
saw Kerrivan and Finn step to the rail of the ship, his first
instinct had been to sound the alarm and warn the sleeping
guards of their escape. He wavered, however, when he thought
about the possibility of finding himself once again in the iron
grip of Finn's massive hands. He had also recognized that this
was an opportunity, as slim as it might be, for he himself to also
make a bolt for freedom.

Thus, within the space of a few seconds, the three men were

in the water, clinging to the large log which they propelled toward shore with their manacled arms and thrusting legs.

When they reached the beach they paused only long enough to let their labored breathing subside for a few seconds before heading off toward the woods that they reckoned lay just beyond the houses and buildings of the settlement. To get there they would have to pass through the community. They prayed that nobody would be awake at this late hour to see them. As they emerged from the icy water, their wet clothes clung to their nearly frozen bodies, chilling them to the bone. Only three weeks earlier this same water had been covered by a massive sheet of slob ice that had moved in with the tide and a strong easterly wind, effectively blocking passage in and out of the harbor for an extended period of time before eventually drifting out again with the tide.

They had no idea where they were going, only that they didn't have a lot of time, for the guards would surely soon awake and find them gone. Perhaps they had already done so. Kerrivan, Finn, and Styles knew that their only chance of success was to put as much distance as possible between themselves and the men who would undoubtedly soon be coming after them, if indeed they had not already begun. And in another couple of hours it would be daylight.

They had no specific plan. When they reached the beginning of the woods without being confronted by anybody, arriving there more by instinct than sight for the morning was still wrapped in blackness, they simply kept going. Inward through the dense woods, away from the coast, feeling their way forward, trying to shield and protect their eyes and faces as best they could from the trees and branches that tore at them in the darkness. With their hands manacled, they were at a terrible disadvantage, yet despite the unrelenting punishment, they kept going. They had no choice.

It was more than two hours later, as the first faint light of dawn was streaking the eastern sky, that they finally emerged from the woods to find themselves facing a great expanse of open wilderness that extended as far as their eyes could see. Their clothing, already much worn and damaged, was by this time in tatters, shredded almost beyond use in their flight through the woods. Their faces, chests, their hands and arms, and virtually every other part of their bodies were scratched and bloodied from the cruel punishment that they had absorbed along the way.

They paused at the outer edge of the woods to catch their breath and to ponder their next move. Finn, who had been following slightly behind Kerrivan for most of the way, came closer and asked, "What do we do now, Peter?"

"I don't know. We can't venture out there in the open, for they'll surely spot us. There's nowhere out there to hide. We'll just have to keep going until we find somewhere to stay until we can figure what to do next."

"What about him?" Finn jerked his thumb over his shoulder toward Styles, who for the entire time since leaving the ship had kept slightly behind the others, keeping just close enough to keep track of the two men ahead of him so that he wouldn't lose them in the darkness. It was the first time that they had acknowledged his presence. Neither of them had yet spoken a word to him.

"I suppose he'll just have to come with us. We can't leave him here, he'll tell the others where we are if they catch him."

"I could take care of him, right here, right now," the big man offered, "then we wouldn't have to worry about him at all."

Kerrivan knew that Finn would do it in an instant if he gave the slightest indication of assent. He considered it briefly, but couldn't bring himself to consent, despite his loathing for the sniveling little man.

"No, let him come with us. If he causes us trouble, we'll deal with him later."

Styles, still keeping his distance, had not actually heard much of the conversation that had taken place between Kerrivan and Finn, but had no misgivings about the gist of what had been said, and knew that he would have to be extremely careful not to do anything that might provoke the anger of either of them.

Kerrivan, who by some tacit understanding had already become the leader of the trio, was still trying to determine their next course of action. They couldn't stay where they were. They had to keep moving, for the men from the *Fortress* might already be close behind.

Then, in the distance, far out in the wilderness, he saw the small mountain, the only high point of land visible for miles. He judged it to be about five or six miles away to the southwest. He remembered hearing somewhere that if you found yourself in trouble, the best thing to do was to head for high ground. His instincts now told him that was good advice.

"I think we'll try to get to that hill out there. At least from there we'd have a good view of anyone approaching across the moor. We'll try to find somewhere to hold up until we can make a break for it."

With Kerrivan in the lead, the three men moved on once more skirting the edge of the woods, making sure that they didn't stray out onto the open barrens where they might risk being seen. After their struggle ashore through the icy waters of the harbor and their brutal trek through the woods, they had little strength to carry on. Each of them knew that if they didn't find a safe hiding place soon they would simply collapse. They pushed on, sometimes half-running, sometimes walking, often barely stumbling along, pausing for a few minutes only when their air-starved lungs would not permit them to take another step.

Finally, an hour later, Kerrivan spotted what he was looking for. Ahead, at the outer edge of the woods, he saw a giant tree, so unlike the others around it that it stood out like a citadel. At least eighty feet high, it was as full and as stately as any oak, elm or chestnut tree that he had ever seen in Ireland or England. The three men paused under the tree for several minutes trying to recover enough strength and energy to climb to its uppermost branches, where they intended to lose themselves in its dense foliage and await a more opportune time to make their bolt for the mountain.

Kerrivan's choice of a hideout would quickly prove to be a good one. They had hardly settled into their perches in the tree before a contingent of men, officers, seamen from the *Fortress*, and soldiers from the garrison, passed within fifty yards as they swept the woods and barrens, searching for them. Late that evening, the same men passed close by again as they returned to the Ferryland Plantation after a full day of fruitless searching.

The three fugitives remained in their hiding place all day until it grew dark. When they did descend, they were somewhat rested and had recovered some of their strength. Although they were anxious to get moving again, they continued to rest and wait beneath the spread of the giant tree until the moon finally rose in the night sky and they could see the faint outline of the mountain in the distance.

They struck out across the barrens. It took them much longer than they had thought it would to cover the relatively short distance to the mountain. With only the moon and the stars to guide them and light their way, they had to claw their way through the tangle of underbrush and alders that lay between themselves and their destination, navigate past the treacherous bogs and quagmires that threatened to suck them to an early and suffocating grave if they erred in their footsteps, and skirt the dozens of small ponds that stood in their way. The tightly matted dwarf ground spruce that covered much of the ground they were traveling over, although only two or three feet in height, impeded their progress most of all. Too springy and too painful to walk over because of its prickly branches, it made them take an erratic zig-zag course that at least doubled the distance they had to cover to reach the mountain.

The new day was breaking when they finally arrived at the base of the mountain. Kerrivan, like Finn and Styles, was so spent and exhausted by the ordeal of his escape and his nocturnal flight across the barrens that he could resist no longer. Almost at the very instant that he hit the ground, he felt the flood of sleep wash sweetly over him.

nine

Captain Smith had spent most of the morning and afternoon in his cabin, trying to keep himself calm by writing dispatches and reading while his officers and seamen were out searching for the escaped prisoners. Several times during the day, whenever he thought about Kerrivan, Finn, and Styles, and the manner of their escape, he had gone on deck and paced furiously until his anger and frustration subsided enough to enable him to focus his mind on other matters. The other men on deck were careful to give him a wide berth.

Smith was especially rankled by the fact that one of the missing men, Kerrivan, had been, albeit very briefly, a member of His Majesty's Royal Navy, and was therefore now a deserter. When he was caught, Smith would see to it that Kerrivan was hanged from the yardarm of the *Fortress* without delay or benefit of further trial.

Earlier in the day, Smith had confined Ensign Sturge to his quarters for his part in the flight of the three men and would make sure when he returned to England that the young ensign would be discharged, or at least demoted, and never serve another day as a naval officer. He knew it was a terrible price for the likeable young man to pay for a few moments of carelessness and indiscretion, and the end of a budding career that might in time have been otherwise brilliant. Still, Smith's inbred sense of justice and discipline compelled him to take this extreme step.

The three negligent seamen were sent to the brig for their part in the fiasco. When they had served their time there, they, unlike Sturge, would be allowed to return to their jobs aboard the ship.

Smith was even more furious when his men returned to the *Fortress* at the end of the day without having recaptured the three escaped prisoners. He made no attempt to mask his anger and made it explicitly clear to the men that he was not pleased with their efforts. Nor was he pleased with himself. This wasn't his style. He realized that he had allowed his frustration and embarrassment to prevail over the calm and controlled manner with which he usually dealt with matters. Yet he couldn't control himself for the moment. His supper churned in his stomach and he knew that he would spend another restless night in his cabin.

The next morning, before sailing to Aquaforte and Fermeuse, he sent them out again. As on the previous day, they were accompanied by eight soldiers from the garrison, the most Lieutenant Stanford could spare. The men from the *Fortress* were told to march the four miles to Fermeuse and rejoin their ship there when they had concluded their search, hopefully with the fugitives in hand.

Smith was waiting for them in Fermeuse when they arrived late that evening after their second full day of searching. He could tell by the slump of their shoulders, their halting pace, and their disgruntled faces, that the men approaching the ship had once again been stymied in their efforts to find the escaped prisoners. And his rage deepened.

The next day he sent them out for the third time – well before first light so that they might have the advantage of surprise on their side. Despite the fact that the men were tired and worn out from their previous two days of slogging through the woods and barrens, he gave them orders to intensify their efforts, and to expand the search area to encompass the mountain in the distance and somewhat beyond. There would be time enough for them to rest once the fugitives had been taken back into custody.

Smith knew that this would be his final attempt to recapture the missing men, for he could not afford to spare any more time on the search and would have to proceed with the rest of his voyage if he were to make it to America and safely back to England in time to avoid the fierce Atlantic storms that autumn and early winter invariably brought with them.

When his men returned to the *Fortress* for the third time empty-handed, he reluctantly accepted the fact that he was beaten. His officers and seamen swore that they had done everything in their power, all that he had ordered them to do and more, and had spared no part of the woods or barrens from their search, including the mountain itself. They had, they told him, scoured every square inch of ground between Ferryland and the mountain, and had left no stone unturned. There was no possible way, they insisted, that they could have missed the three fugitives if they had indeed been anywhere within the area that they had covered.

Satisfied that he himself had also done everything possible, but knowing that he would nevertheless suffer this humiliation to the end of his days, he then ordered the *Fortress* to be prepared for sea and set sail for America, effectively leaving the matter of the three men in the wilderness in the hands of Lieutenant Stanford.

ten

From their vantage point at the base of the mountain, Kerrivan, Finn, and Styles had been able to observe their pursuers in the distance as they swept across the barrens, fanned out to effectively cover as large an area as possible. It was on the second day of their arrival on the mountain, early in the morning, that they had actually spied Smith's men for the first time. They had been lucky. Having slept through the entire previous day, so exhausted by their ordeal that they simply couldn't stay awake or keep moving any longer despite knowing full well that Smith would have his men out combing the woods and wilderness for them, they were fortunate that the searchers had concentrated most of their initial efforts on the coast and the woods. When they eventually moved out onto the open barrens, they did not advance quite as far as the mountain, having had only enough time to investigate the many intervening wales and scattered patches of forestation before having to retreat again at dusk.

Despite their narrow escape, Kerrivan realized that Smith would not rest until his officers and men had exhausted all possibilities, and that he, Finn, and Styles would need to devise some sort of escape plan for the assault on the mountain that they all knew inevitably must come.

They also had two other pressing priorities. They were starving. The few small trout that Finn had been able to fling out of a small bog hole with his bare hands after almost two hours of trying were all that they had eaten since escaping from the ship. And secondly, if they were to have any chance of survival at all, they must rid themselves of the manacles that inhibited their movements at every turn.

By early afternoon, food was still a problem. They had,

however, finally been successful in shedding their manacles. Finn, with his almost superhuman strength, had ground and beaten at their chains with heavy rocks and sharp stones until they were weakened enough for him to pry them apart with his massive hands.

The wrists and hands of all three men had been severely bruised and chafed raw in the process. Their feet were sore and blistered, and the remnants of what once were boots did little or nothing to protect them. The lacerations and contusions that they had incurred in the woods, although mostly superficial, caused them great pain, and the welts that they had received from their lashings only two weeks earlier had not yet fully healed. But despite their hunger and extreme discomfort, they were still on their feet.

Taking great care not to expose themselves to the men in the distance, Kerrivan, Finn, and Styles spent the rest of the day exploring the slopes and the upper reaches of the mountain, searching for a suitable place of concealment, somewhere where they would not only be safer from the prying eyes of their pursuers but also a place where they might be able to sleep more comfortably and keep themselves warm. For out in the wilderness of the Southern Shore in May, no matter how warm the day might be, the temperature at night invariably plummets, sometimes to the freezing point or even lower, as they had found out on their first night there.

They discovered that the small mountain on which they stood contained numerous clusters of large boulders, many hollows and indentations, and patches of dense spruce, but nothing, however, that would effectively provide them the protection that they were looking for. Discouraged by what they found, they quickly reached the conclusion that their only recourse if and when their pursuers came, was to continue to flee further westward into the wilderness. Hopefully, they would be able to see them approaching in time to give themselves a good head start.

On the third day the assault came. It came so suddenly and so early in the morning that Kerrivan, Finn, and Styles had to abandon their contingency plan to continue westward, for they knew, as before, that out on the open barrens, without a good lead, they would surely be spotted and hounded until they were eventually brought to earth. Certain that their pursuers had not yet spotted them, they began a hasty and unplanned retreat up onto the mountain, veering southward and upward on a path that would eventually bring them near the top of the mountain, on its western side, as far removed from their pursuers as possible in the circumstances.

They could hear the voices of the men following them as they came closer. The officers in charge had again deployed their men strategically to cover as much ground as possible in the shortest amount of time, spreading them out until there was a space of only a hundred yards or less between the searchers as they converged toward the top of the mountain, scouring every inch of the terrain that they passed over.

Kerrivan, Finn, and Styles continued their frantic scramble upward, trying desperately to stay out of the line of sight of their pursuers by keeping to the trees and boulders, being careful as they did so to leave no visible trail that might give away their presence on the mountain. Despite their exhausted state, fear and desperation drove them onward. Although they realized that as they climbed higher and higher their options were quickly running out, they had no other choice. They could tell by the shouts and yells below that their pursuers had already substantially closed the distance between them.

Finally, as they neared the top of the mountain, Kerrivan, Finn, and Styles conceded the fact that their luck had finally run out. There were no more trees or boulders that they might hide behind. The only thing that now stood between them and the top of the mountain was the steep twenty-foot escarpment of rock that rose directly in front of them. With nowhere else to go and knowing that they had only seconds before their pursuers broke through the small ring of trees behind them, the three men quickly scaled the rock, their desperate fingers and feet finding enough crevices and footholds in the cliff to take them to the top before their pursuers arrived. They were at the end of the line. They knew it would now be only a matter of time before they were discovered and recaptured.

When they reached the top, however, they couldn't quite believe what they found. For directly behind the top of the escarpment, completely out of the vision of anyone standing at its base, was a shallow, bowl-like fissure in the rock, large enough to hold all three of them, undoubtedly gouged out by some glacier millions of years earlier. It was filled with dark, freezing water that had undoubtedly lain there since that time, replenished whenever it rained or snowed. Unless the men following them actually scaled the escarpment as they themselves had done, neither the fissure itself nor anyone hiding in it could be detected from below on either side of the mountain.

And thanks again to the laxness of His Majesty's Royal Navy, their luck held. Only minutes after Kerrivan, Finn, and Styles had settled into their watery hideaway in the top of the rock, Able Seaman Sidney Inkster arrived at the base of the cliff directly below them. The young sailor whose rubbery legs were more accustomed to the rolling deck of the *Fortress* than to the three days of heavy slogging through the woods and the barrens he had just done, took one look at the sheer cliff and could not summon up the final reserve of energy to climb the last twenty feet to the top. Instead, from where he stood, he eyed the wall of granite for several minutes until he finally convinced himself that there was no possible way that anyone could be up there.

Later, when the searchers reassembled at the base of the mountain with nothing but sweat and frustration to show for their efforts, the officers conferred and concluded that the three escaped prisoners that they were searching for could not possibly be on the mountain, and that they had undoubtedly fled into the wilderness to the west – or perhaps had never been on the mountain in the first place.

eleven

errivan, Finn, and Styles did not come down from their perch on top of the mountain until long after they were certain that the searchers had left. When they did, wet and stiff, they descended slowly and very cautiously in case Smith's men had left a rearguard or had set some sort of trap or pitfall for them. Having been taken by surprise once, they vowed that they would never be caught off guard again. They agreed that they would take turns keeping watch, day and night, no matter what the weather or how tired or worn out they might be.

Their next few days at the base of the mountain were spent trying to recover from their ordeal. Their state of near starvation was still their most pressing concern, for other than the trout in the small pond, they had so far been unable to find anything else in the way of food or nourishment. It was still too early in the year for berries or wild fruit of any kind. Even the alders did not yet have their new leaves. The only other leafy vegetation around was the inedible goowithy itself. Gaunt and often lightheaded from their prolonged hunger, the men were growing weaker by the day.

Kerrivan and Finn had paid little attention to Styles since the three of them had left the ship together. They scarcely acknowledged his presence other than to give him some order or to snarl at him for some reason, deserved or otherwise. Styles wisely kept his peace and his distance, knowing full well that his tolerated presence here with the other two men was tenuous at best.

Despite his lowly standing with them, he was, ironically, the first to make a meaningful contribution toward improving their dire circumstances. His many years of poaching on the large protected estates of English gentlemen, where he had relieved the wealthy owners of many of their salmon, deer, hares, and other types of wildlife, a crime for which he had twice been caught and punished, now paid off. When his experienced eyes spied the almost indistinguishable network of tiny paths and runs among the gorse and the alders, which neither Kerrivan nor Finn would have ever noticed no matter how long they might have looked, he realized that the area around the base of the mountain on which they were standing was a virtual rabbit warren. He suspected that other small animals, perhaps foxes or squirrels, as well as ground birds like grouse or pheasant, also inhabited the area.

Without telling the others, he fashioned a number of slips[3] from his bootlaces and thin strips of cloth torn from his shirt, and set them in what he thought might be the most promising places among the gorse and alders, and waited.

The next morning Kerrivan and Finn were sitting close to a small fire trying to dispel the chill of the cold night that they had passed in the open, covered only by a few boughs, when Styles brought them breakfast – two plump hares. It was the first meat that the men had eaten in more than a week, and the first of the many fat rabbits that would form an important part of their diet for years to come.

Styles, too, was the one who found the shelter that they had all searched for, and missed, earlier. Or rather, he had stumbled onto it. On his hands and knees, as he was trying to follow a particular animal run that seemed to hold more potential than the others, he had almost fallen into it before he had actually seen it – a large indentation in the vertical wall of sheer rock that rose at one point from the base of the mountain.

It was not quite deep enough to be considered a cave, but certainly deep enough to provide some overhead shelter from the rain and snow, and a place where the men would be able to sleep in relative comfort with at least some semblance of protection from the elements. And even more importantly, it was fronted by a thicket of small spruce trees and alders so densely interwoven that it made an almost impenetrable wall that would shield them from the weather – or even prying eyes.

---

[3] Snares

The existence of the indentation in the rock could not be detected from any angle within a radius of a hundred feet or more, and unless someone stumbled upon it by accident, as Styles had done, it was completely hidden, virtually invisible. It was also close enough to the lookout spot where they would each take their turn on watch to enable anyone waiting there to hear the warning signal if given by the man on duty. It was perfect, exactly what they had been searching for.

With their hunger assuaged, at least temporarily, the three men continued their search for food and, over the next few days, despite the fact that most of the slips that they set were so flimsy that they broke with even the slightest strain, they were successful in catching a few more rabbits. They were also fortunate enough to snare a partridge, one of several that they had seen and heard in the area. Then Finn had come upon a second partridge wandering aimlessly over the barrens, extremely fat and not overly perturbed by his presence, which after a short attempt at flight fell to the ground and could go no further because of its overweight condition, and the big man killed it easily with a stick.

Then, when halfway up the southern slope of the mountain, they discovered an abundant supply of large eggs, not yet hatched, which they believed were laid there by gulls from the coast, Kerrivan, Finn, and Styles realized that the bounty of the Butterpot mountain, if they looked closely enough to see it, could sustain them for quite some time. To make their prospects even brighter, a week later they spotted the first of the great herd of caribou that roamed the area at the time. Although at first they had no means of catching any of these large animals, after several days of trying they finally managed to stalk one that had strayed from the main herd and shepherded it into a small enclosed gully, where they killed it with stones and cudgels broken from a nearby spruce tree, and dragged it back to the indentation in the cliff. Later they would devise more effective traps and strategies to catch these animals, and the rich meat would become the dominant part of their future diet. The hides of the slaughtered animals would also help keep them warm and protected from the elements.

As the three men slowly recovered their strength and

regained some of the weight that they had lost, Kerrivan turned his thoughts to the string of settlements on the nearby coast. Each day he would climb partway up the mountain, sometimes to the very top, and spend an hour or two surveying them in the distance. The settlement furthest to the northeast, he realized, was the one through which he, Finn, and Styles had passed while making their escape from the *Fortress*. The next one, a little further south, was the closest to them. He judged it to be four or five miles away. He didn't know then that another small community, nestled in a deep fiord-like indentation in the coast and completely hidden from his view-point on the mountain, lay between these two. Still further south, perhaps another four or five miles, he could faintly see what he assumed to be the houses of yet another village.

In time, he and the other members of the band would come to know that the names of the settlements on the stretch of coastline that he was viewing were the Ferryland Plantation, Aquaforte, Fermeuse, and Renews respectively. Cappahayden, four miles further south of Renews, another settlement that would over the next few years feel the impact of Kerrivan and his men, could not, like Aquaforte, be seen from the mountain.

After deliberating on the matter for some time, Kerrivan made his first foray into the settlements, taking Finn with him. He chose a clear moonlit night so that they might make their way across the barrens without too much difficulty. The much despised Styles was left behind, for Kerrivan's distrust of the little man was still too great to risk taking him along. He selected as his target the settlement of Fermeuse, the one closest to them.

By the time they made their way into the settlement, the residents of its twenty or so dwellings had mostly retired for the night, and Kerrivan and Finn had almost the full run of the tiny sleeping settlement. Only the baying of a dog somewhere in the farthest end of the settlement, perhaps the only creature in the entire community that was aware of their presence, disturbed their stealthy progress through its single narrow road. Still, the pickings were scant, for the people of the settlement, among the poorest on this stretch of coastline, always kept anything of even the slightest value locked up or inside with them.

Nevertheless, when the two men finally made their way

back to the Butterpot mountain several hours later, they brought back with them a number of items that would help make their lot in the wilderness a little easier. The discarded piece of fishing net that someone had left to rot on the top of a fence post would prove invaluable for catching trout from the pond. The length of fishing twine that they brought back would serve to make better, stronger and more effective slips than they had been able to fashion out of their bootlaces and pieces of their clothing, and a large often patched and much mended quilt that some man or woman had left drying on the grass would keep at least one of them a little warmer at night.

As uneventful as the raid had been, it marked the beginning of an assault on the settlements that would continue for a number of years. Emboldened by the relative success of their first foray, Kerrivan pondered his next venture. This time he thought he would try the settlement a little further to the south (Renews), hoping it might be a little larger than the first and yield them more things of value than they had gotten in Fermeuse.

Before embarking on the raid, however, he thought it might be prudent if he first reconnoitered the settlement by himself, reasoning that if he had some idea of the size and layout of the settlement and what it contained beforehand, he and Finn should be able to make the most of their limited time there, and have a planned escape route in case they had to make a hasty retreat back to the mountain.

After telling the others of his intentions, Kerrivan crossed the barrens once again. This time he did not bother to wait for darkness but left late in the afternoon, despite the risk that he might be seen by somebody in the open wilderness area. The previous trek that he and Finn had made across the barrens in the darkness, even in the fullness of the moon, had been much more arduous than either of them had expected, and taken them much longer than they had anticipated. He now reasoned that even if he were spotted, it would be no serious matter because he already concluded that most of the settlers in the area suspected that he and his companions were out there somewhere in the wilderness anyway.

An hour later, having crossed the barrens and while progressing along the fringe of forest that lay between the barrens

and the settlements on the coast, he passed the large oak tree that he, Finn, and Styles had hidden in during their escape, and gave it a grateful glance as he went by. A short distance further along, he found a well-worn footpath into the woods that he thought might lead him into the settlement. He followed it, taking care to travel as quietly as possible to avoid being seen or heard. The gurgling of the small river that ran alongside the path for most of the way suddenly reminded him of the River Foyle, momentarily taking him back more than twenty years.

About half a mile into the woods, he suddenly found himself in a clearing in the middle of which stood a crude hut made of logs. It was one of the most unsightly structures that he had ever seen, even worse than the shelter in Osbern's Blind, and he wondered briefly what purpose it served. Then, standing in the far edge of the clearing in the soft twilight of the evening, with her arms resting on her shovel, obviously taking a breather from her labors, he spotted a woman. He noted that she was very thin and taller than any other woman he had ever seen.

There did not seem to be anyone else around. He watched the woman for a few minutes, wondering why she was there all alone in the middle of the woods. Could it be possible that she lived here? For even as he stood there, the faint smell of wood-smoke passed his nostrils. When the woman, unaware of his presence, resumed her work, he proceeded again on his journey into the settlement, still puzzled. It was the first time that he laid eyes on the woman who would play an integral role in the sequence of events that would ensue over the coming months and years.

It was dusk when the footpath that he was following finally brought him into the settlement. He decided to wait until it was fully dark before proceeding any further. From his position, where the river flowed into the harbor, he could see that the settlement was, as he had hoped, much larger than the first one they had raided. He estimated that it had thirty or more houses, and the beaches on both sides of the harbor were dotted with wharves, fishing rooms, and drying platforms. The harbor itself appeared to be very shallow as large rocks broke the surface in many places.

He realized that he would have to wait until most of its residents had settled in for the night before entering the settlement. He could hear the voices of men and women still at work, and the shouts and laughter of children spending a last few minutes at play before being put to bed for the night. When he finally left his vantage point an hour later, lamps were still burning in a few of the houses, and he proceeded very cautiously, ready to retreat at a moment's notice if anybody challenged him. As he stole around the settlement, he quickly realized, however, that the purpose of his visit, to assess the potential of the settlement, would go unfulfilled that night because he could see no further than a few yards in the darkness. He would have to come back another time, in better light.

His journey back to the mountain took him past the log hut in the clearing again, and he wondered if the woman was asleep inside. There was no light in the hut to indicate her presence, but the smell of wood-fire still hung in the cool night air.

Two weeks later, he tried again. This time in broad daylight. He simply walked into Renews one morning and wandered around its roads and lanes as if he lived there. Incredibly, despite his tattered clothes and his fierce, unkempt appearance, nobody challenged him or accosted him in any manner. He was free to walk around the settlement as he wished. In fact, a few people bid him good-day or nodded to him as they passed. Not a single person who saw him, in the entire settlement, had entertained the thought that one of the outlaws in the wilderness would have the audacity to come into their presence and walk around their community as if he were one of them. Perhaps they thought that he was one of the indentured men from the Ferryland Plantation or from one of the other nearby settlements, or simply some stranger passing through. They didn't realize that Kerrivan, as he walked among them, was taking note of many items that would, over the coming weeks and months, find their way one by one back to the Butterpot mountain.

Each time he traveled back and forth between Renews and the mountain, whether alone or with Finn, he paused for a few minutes to watch the tall woman at her work. He concluded by now that she lived there by herself in the clearing in the woods.

twelve

B y the time spring passed into summer, life for the outlaws in the wilderness had improved substantially. They now had enough to eat on most days, and were warm and secure in the indentation in the cliff. On a number of occasions they had spotted the advance of large groups of men, obviously sent in search of them, in time to hide themselves and avoid being captured. And the barrens themselves were already covered with millions of tiny white berries that within a month or so would ripen, turn a deep powdery blue, and provide a succulent complement to their predominantly meat diet.

Then, in the middle of July, the ranks of the tiny band of outlaws on the Butterpot was increased by the unexpected arrival of two newcomers, the Shannahan brothers, John and Liam, escaped prisoners from the Ferryland Plantation, who one day had fled from the garrison in a moment when their guardians were distracted by a more pressing matter.

Fifteen years earlier, the two brothers had been hunted down and arrested in Belfast, Ireland, and subsequently sentenced to twenty years imprisonment each for their part in a failed uprising against their English overlords. John, the older of the two, was twenty-four years of age at the time. Liam was two years younger. Fortunately for the brothers, their roles in the plot had been considered by the judges who tried them to have been relatively minor in comparison to the others involved and they were spared the harsher penalty of hanging.

The leaders of the revolt had not been so lucky. Nine of them were publicly hanged en masse early one morning while a sullen, angry gathering of their fellow Irish compatriots looked on, shouting words of comfort and encouragement to the doomed men while they directed curses and obscenities at their

English executioners. Only the presence of a hundred or more heavily armed English soldiers had prevented the assembly from escalating into a bloody, full-scale riot, for every Irish man and woman there considered the executions of the nine men to be yet another example of British brutality and overkill. To inflict the ultimate indignity upon the situation, the hanged men had been left dangling on their ropes for the rest of the day as a warning to any other Irish men and women who might be contemplating rebellion against English rule. It was almost midnight before the bodies of the men were finally cut down and turned over to their relatives and friends for burial.

The Shannahans had served the first twelve years of their sentence in prison in London where they, like Kerrivan and Finn, had labored each day in the stone quarry and survived in the brutal environment of the prison by keeping their own counsel and looking after and protecting each other in much the same manner as Kerrivan and Finn were at the same time doing in Queenshythe Prison. Still, the life of confinement did not sit well with the brothers, especially John, who over and over again, during his frequent bouts of depression, would tell Liam that he preferred to be dead.

"I'd rather be crucified on a cross like the Blessed Saviour than spend one more day under the heel of the English dogs. I wish He'd take me right now," he would often moan, or, as he sometimes did, lapse into a period of weeping and frustration so intense that he was scarcely aware of his brother at his side trying to console him.

All attempts by Liam to give solace to his older brother when he was depressed were futile, and John's bouts of depression simply had to run their course. Invariably, however, after a few hours of introspective desolation, John would somehow summon up the will to pull himself out of his despair and continue on. Hope of escape from the prison was the motivation that kept him, as well as Liam, going, for the love of freedom and independence from their hated English rulers still burned as deeply as ever within their Irish souls.

Despite their loathing for their captors and their constant intent on escape, the brothers somehow managed to keep themselves from becoming embroiled in any serious incidents within the prison, and as time passed they came to be considered model prisoners by the administrators of the prison and the jailers who watched over them.

When, in the thirteenth year of their imprisonment, they were told that, because of their good records, they were being transferred to spend the remainder of their sentences as laborers on a plantation in Newfoundland, they couldn't quite believe their good fortune. Anything would be better than the suffocating, cold gray walls of the prison and the dirty backbreaking toil that they were required to do every day in the quarry. At least they might once again be able to breath the fresh outdoor air and know the feel of the wind on their faces and the warmth of the sun on their bodies.

As they had anticipated, their lot in the Ferryland Plantation was a dramatic improvement over their nightmare existence in the prison. While they still had to work every bit as hard as they had in jail, their tasks were now more varied and were mostly done in the fresh outdoor air that had been denied to them for so long.

One of the jobs for which they were ideally suited because of their many years of practice at swinging a sledgehammer in the prison quarry, was wood cutting. The two brothers were therefore almost always included whenever a detail of men was selected and sent to the nearby forest to cut timber or firewood for the plantation. They also spent endless hours in the garrison's two-man saw pit turning the logs that they brought back to the garrison into long planks for construction work and repairs or into shorter lengths for burning. They tended the plantation's vegetable gardens in the summer and shoveled snow in the winter. And, without complaint, did every other task that was assigned to them, no matter what it entailed.

Lieutenant Stanford, despite the cruel nature of his personality, knew that a machine works best when it is well maintained, and that the survival of the plantation depended in no small measure on the free labor provided by its prisoners and indentured men and women. It was, therefore, even though he saw them as little more than draught animals, clearly to his advantage as the senior ranking person in the area, to keep them all as healthy and as strong as possible.

So the Shannahan brothers, like the others, were well fed, twice a day on a diet that almost always included a serving of meat, usually salted beef or pork, but fresh meat too when it was available, as well as bread, vegetables, berries or wild fruit and as much hot tea as they wanted. A far cry from the thin gruel that they had been fed in prison. Incredibly, the brothers were even occasionally slipped a jug of ale or a tot of dark rum by the guards with whom they had gradually developed a kind of grudging rapport. And they slept in a warm bed each night.

The Shannahan brothers, for the first time in many years, were relaxed and perhaps even a bit contented in their environment, and the details of the revolt in which they had participated many years earlier were now but dim memories in the background of their minds. Security at the under-manned plantation was much laxer than it had been in the prison, yet the brothers had repeatedly passed up on numerous opportunities for escape that they would have seized upon without a second's thought a few years earlier. They had only a relatively short time left to serve in their sentences. They even harbored some hope that their sentences might yet be commuted on the basis of their continued good behavior.

And then they heard the stories that were circulating around the plantation about the wild men living out on the barrens. They, like everybody else in the settlement, had heard about the escape of the three men from the *Fortress* shortly after it had occurred. While the incident had caused a stir in the plantation for a few days, it was soon forgotten in the midst of other things, and life for the Shannahans and the other prisoners returned to normal.

Gradually, however, as the weeks of spring and summer passed, rumors persistently drifted back to the ears of the brothers that the men who had escaped were still within the area, living somewhere out in the wilderness. Some said that they had a hideout on the Butterpot mountain so secluded and impregnable that no attempt to find and recapture them could possibly succeed. There were stories of raids by the outlaws into some of the other nearby settlements, and sightings of unknown sinister men were reported almost every week by some of the settlers in the area.

As they listened to these rumors and stories, the Shannahan brothers' passion for freedom was rekindled. Despite the fact that they had by now served most of their time, they simply could not push from their minds the thought of the other men, convicts like themselves, living freely out on the barrens, and they once again began to look for an opportunity to escape. For they had already, almost without conscious thought and without much discussion having passed between them on the matter, resolved to find the outlaws if they possibly could and join them in their wilderness hideout.

They knew where the Butterpot was located, for they had seen the small mountain in the distance one day when one of their wood cutting expeditions had taken them out to the edge of the barren wilderness. For them, it was now only a matter of biding their time for the right moment.

The escape opportunity that they were waiting for was not long in coming. Late one afternoon in the following week, as they were taking their regular shift in the saw pit, John and Liam heard the cry, "Fire! Fire!" that immediately sent everyone in the garrison running toward the section of barracks from which dark, dense smoke was already beginning to billow. Fire was one of the greatest fears of the people who lived in the settlements along the coast (as indeed was the case everywhere else in Newfoundland), for with nothing more than buckets and pails, they had no way to effectively battle any fire once it had gained momentum. Most of their efforts in such situations were directed as much at wetting down other nearby houses and outbuildings to try to prevent them too from being destroyed as they were at trying to extinguish the original fire itself.

Every man, woman and child within earshot automatically and immediately, when the warning was sounded, converged on the scene of a blaze, knowing full well that even the tiniest flame, once fanned by the ocean winds and breezes that continually swirled around the settlements of the coast, could develop into a raging inferno within the matter of a few short minutes.

When Liam, his body covered by sawdust from several hours of sawing, climbed out of the pit and started to follow the others to the location of the fire, John grabbed his arm and held him back. "Liam, this is it. We'll never have a better chance than this."

It took a few seconds for Liam to comprehend the meaning of his brother's words. When he did, he simply put on the shirt that he had taken off a few hours earlier and, without hesitation, followed his brother over the garrison wall, both of them gambling that the attention of the soldier on guard at the garrison gate would be focused on the fire inside.

It took the men of the garrison two hours to get the fire under control. By that time, the section of barracks in which the fire had originated was reduced to ashes and the sections adjacent to it were blackened and scorched, although still standing. They would be reusable once they were cleaned up and aired out for a few days. It took at least another hour for the men to clear away some of the smoking debris and put out the hot spots that continued to flare up every few minutes. It was not until the garrison had gradually returned to some semblance of normality and the prisoners and the others had been called to their supper, that the absence of the Shannahan brothers was discovered. By then, with a head start of several hours, the two men were already well across the open barrens on their way to the Butterpot mountain.

Ned Finn, whose turn it was to stand watch, spotted the brothers when they were still mere specks in the distance. He thought at first that they were animals, perhaps sheep or goats that had strayed from one of the settlements on the coast, but as they came closer he realized that they were men. He watched them for several minutes before concluding that the course they were following across the barrens would eventually bring them close to the spot where he was standing. They seemed to be coming at a fast pace and had already covered at least three-quarters of the distance to the mountain. He gave a soft whistle, the agreed upon warning sign, and a few seconds later Kerrivan appeared at his side.

"Peter, what do you make of that?"

Kerrivan, whose eyesight was not as keen as Finn's, could not at first see the men in the distance until Finn pointed them out to him.

Styles, curious to see what was happening, had joined Finn and Kerrivan as they continued to watch the approaching men. His own sharp eyes had picked up the two men immediately.

"I wonder who they are?" he wondered aloud, "Do you think they might be looking for us?"

Kerrivan thought that there was something odd about the way the two men were approaching. The fact that they continued to look back over their shoulders every few seconds indicated that someone might be following them, although Kerrivan could see nobody else on the barrens. The men appeared to be in considerable distress. Even as he watched, he saw the man in the rear stumble and fall, and despite his efforts to regain his feet, stay down until the other man went back and helped him to his feet again.

Even though the men appeared to be alone and unarmed, Kerrivan was worried. "There's only the two of them and they've brought nothing with them that I can see. I think they're running from something. Stay here out of sight, and we'll just wait and see what they're up to."

Within the space of another twenty minutes, the two men were nearing the base of the mountain. The trailing man fell again, for the third time, and this time made no effort at all to rise to his feet despite the frantic urging of his companion who finally half carried and half dragged him until he, too, dropped – not more than a hundred yards from the very spot where Kerrivan, Finn, and Styles themselves had collapsed after their own flight across the barrens two months earlier.

Still cautious, Kerrivan ordered Finn and Styles to wait. "Leave them there. There's no need to hurry, they're not going anywhere."

And Kerrivan, Finn, and Styles waited – until it was dusk and they were satisfied that the two men had not been followed across the barrens. Leaving Styles to nevertheless keep a lookout, Kerrivan and Finn finally left their hiding place and went to confront the two men now lying prostrate in the brush.

John Shannahan was spent from his nine-mile trek through the woods and across the barrens, but, unlike his brother, was still partly awake. He knew nothing until a deep guttural growl brought him to his senses.

"Make one move and I'll break your bloody neck."

When he opened his eyes and saw the massive bulk of Ned Finn standing over him and felt the weight of the man's big foot planted firmly in the middle of his chest, he knew that any attempt at resistance would be certain suicide. A few paces away, Kerrivan stood over Liam, who had long since lapsed into the deep sleep of sheer exhaustion.

"Liam, wake up. We're there, we've found them. Or they've found us."

A few sharp nudges of Kerrivan's boot did what John Shannahan's words couldn't, and Liam slowly opened his eyes, blinked several times, wondered for a few moments where he was, and then sat bolt upright.

Kerrivan spoke to them for the first time. "Who the devil are you?"

The older brother spoke for both of them. "I'm John Shannahan. This is my brother Liam. We've just come from the garrison in Ferryland. There was a fire, and we left in the confusion. I'm sure they'll be coming after us as soon as they know we're gone."

Kerrivan wasn't satisfied. "How do we know you are what you say you are? And why in bloody hell did you choose to come here?"

As John stared into the intense blue eyes that seemed to pass right through him, he wanted to somehow tell the tall blond man about the bizarre sequence of events that had now finally brought him and his brother to this sorry plight, and of his loathing for the English, and all the passion and frustration that had been bottled up inside him for so many years. But he couldn't find the words. Instead, he simply replied, "We came to try to find you. Don't turn us away. We've nowhere else to go. We can't go back. They'll surely send us back to prison in England – or hang us."

The mention of prison, ironically, eased some of Kerrivan's suspicions. And when the two brothers described in livid detail the deprivation and hardship that they had experienced in the London prison, and told him about the cruel and sadistic actions of the jailers and the other prisoners, and their back-breaking work in the quarry, Kerrivan knew from his own experience that the brothers had told the truth. And John and Liam Shannahan were welcomed into the small outlaw band, the first of many other men who would follow.

thirteen

By the end of their first summer in the wilderness, the existence of the outlaw band, now numbering five men, was no longer a secret to anyone in the area. It was confirmed by the continuous spate of thefts that plagued each of the five settlements, and Kerrivan and the other members of the band had been sighted so often and in so many different places that many of the settlers could describe them with accurate detail. The victimized settlers, especially those of Renews, had complained on several occasions to Lieutenant Stanford in the Ferryland garrison, who assured them that he was doing everything within his power to find and apprehend the outlaws.

Not all of the robberies could in truth be laid solely at the feet of the outlaws. For some settlers, the more unscrupulous and dishonest, of which each of the afflicted settlements had its share, took advantage of the opportunity to steal from their neighbors with impunity, knowing that the outlaws in the wilderness would almost certainly shoulder the blame. To the outlaws' credit, there had not been, at least so far, any wanton property damage or bodily harm to any individual. That would come later.

Kerrivan liked the cooler September air. The month of August had been exceptionally hot and the nights in the indentation in the cliff had been muggy and uncomfortable. Nevertheless, the summer had been good to him and his companions as they gorged themselves on the blueberries, wild raspberries, cloudberries, black currents and other delicacies that grew in abundance in the area around the base of the Butterpot mountain.

Their raids into the settlements netted them many items that helped make their existence in the wilderness a little more palatable. The first of the salted codfish that they had stolen from flakes and drying racks had touched their palates and sent them back time after time for more. They also had, by now, bedding enough to discard the boughs that they had used to cover themselves while they slept. They were even able to replace their tattered and ragged clothes with others pilfered from clotheslines from Ferryland to Cappahayden. The few implements that they accumulated included knives, buckets, and a small saw. On one occasion, Finn even brought back with him a keg of ale that he had discovered fermenting in some settler's shed, and he and the other members of the band had drunk themselves into oblivion for the first time in years. It was also the first time since their arrival there several months earlier that they had let down their guard and did not have someone posted on look-out. Fortunately, nobody had chosen that moment to come searching for them. Their most important prize, although it would be useless to them until they were able to acquire powder and shot for it months later, was a flintlock musket that someone had momentarily left unattended. Its value would eventually manifest itself many times over in their continuing quest for caribou meat to feed themselves.

Ever fearful of another surprise attack by the soldiers of the garrison, the outlaws established three other hiding places to which they could retreat if the need arose. They also established a network of false trails and diversions to lead searchers away from any of their hideout locations.

The Shannahan brothers were a good addition to the band. They fitted in well, and with their increased numbers, it was now a little easier for the members of the band to keep up their constant vigilance against attack. Kerrivan and Finn both liked the company of the two brothers from Ireland and enjoyed the endless stories that they told around their campfire each night. Sometimes, after listening to the Shannahans spin their patriotic tales, Finn, an Englishman himself, was so sympathetic to the cause of the poor downtrodden Irish the Shannahans described that he too began to develop a great dislike for the brutal English overlords who ruled Ireland so ruthlessly and the greedy absentee English landowners who exploited the impoverished Irish men, women, and children so badly.

Only Styles was left out. Despite the fact that he had been the first one to find food, stood his watch as faithfully and as regularly as the rest of them, and did his fair share of everything else, he was still a misfit, a pariah within the band. Even the newcomers, especially John Shannahan, had as little to do with him as possible. Sometimes, when he dwelled on his unhappy circumstances, Styles regretted that he had ever escaped from the *Fortress* and come out here in the first place. Now only the fear of the rope kept him from going back. But here, even if he didn't have companionship, he at least had food and shelter.

The band had no specific structure. Kerrivan was its undisputed leader. It was he who assigned watch duty, and it was he who organized and led the band's forays into the settlements. None of the others ever openly questioned his leadership. Twice, when the band had made forays into Renews and passed by the crude log hut in the clearing in the woods where the tall woman lived alone, some of the other men had wanted to drop in to see her. Kerrivan, who had watched her surreptitiously on several subsequent occasions since that first time in the clearing, told them all about her. Both times, however, knowing what the inevitable outcome of such a visit would be, he stopped them. The steely glint of his intense blue eyes had deterred the men from pressing the matter any further. Kerrivan already felt a strange kinship with the woman who, like himself, appeared to be an outcast in the wilderness.

Even though there had been no intentional attempt on the part of Kerrivan, or by any of the other men for that matter, to structure the band's activities in any manner, they had nevertheless unconsciously slipped into a routine that served to give the band at least a modicum of organization. Every night, as they sat around the fire, they would invariably discuss their situation and circumstances, exchange thoughts and ideas on things that they needed and things that needed to be done, and plot their next raid.

It was during one such campfire gathering that Styles, the Snitch, uttered the words that would immortalize the outlaw band in the minds of countless future generations of Newfoundlanders. John Shannahan, having become sad and morose, as he was sometimes wont to do when telling his stories about Ireland, opined that, "Here we are out here by ourselves, without a bit of property or chick or child to call our own, with the law breathing down our necks all the time, ready to hang us all in a minute if they could. But, for all that, we might just as easily have all been fine gentlemen of society if we had only been given a chance, or done things a little differently."

Even though Styles always listened to whatever was being discussed and enjoyed the stories and tales of the Shannahans as much as the others, he seldom participated in any of the discussions or offered any thoughts or suggestions of his own. Nor did he complain, for he thought it best in the circumstances to keep his problems to himself. On this occasion, however, his deep-felt frustration got the best of him and prompted him to speak out.

"Society be damned. And gentlemen too. We're a bleeding society unto ourselves out here. We make our own laws, and we don't have to answer to anyone else. A society of masterless men, that's what we are. And may the rest of them all rot in hell, the whole bloody lot."

And these words, coined in scorn and sarcasm, would outlive the little man who uttered them by hundreds of years.

Cool September blended into an even cooler October, and the days grew shorter and the nights a little longer. Kerrivan realized too late that they had missed the opportunity to cache some of the fruit of the barrens for the coming winter, for by the time the idea finally occurred to him the berries had already fallen, and the band would have to survive their first winter in the wilderness on a diet consisting mostly of the caribou, rabbits, and partridge that populated the area on a year-round basis. He did, however, think about stockpiling some firewood for the colder months that he knew lay ahead. The men also learned from experience that dried wood, dead-fall, was the best for burning in their fires because of its thin blueish smoke. Greener wood, particularly freshly cut boughs, was the worse, for the billowing black smoke that it gave off could be seen for miles and might betray the location of their hideout to anyone who saw it.

Still, despite the lateness of the season, Kerrivan and the other men were comfortable in their surroundings. The heavy dew and occasional hoarfrost that covered the ground most mornings were usually quickly dissipated by the warming sun, and the heavy rains that were sometimes driven across the open barrens in blinding sheets by the fierce autumn winds could not penetrate the dense wall of trees and shrubbery in front of the indentation in the cliff, and the men waited inside in dry comfort.

The favorable weather continued into early November. The outlaws continued to carry out their random raids into the villages, each time frustrating the authorities who tried in vain to anticipate their moves. To Kerrivan and his companions, it became almost a game. Sometimes they would deliberately make themselves visible to the settlers to flaunt and tease them. Still, they always took the precaution of returning to the mountain by a circuitous route, and were careful to never leave a trail behind that anyone could follow.

Before the end of the year, two events, seemingly inconsequential at the time, occurred that would have a profound impact on the destiny of the outlaw band.

The first took place one night in the second week of November when, after the men had dozed off one by one inside the indentation in the cliff, the temperature outside suddenly plummeted below the freezing point and snow began to fall. When Finn awoke in the early hours of the morning, he was so cold that he resisted going out of the indentation to empty his bladder, as he did on most nights, for as long as possible. Finally, he could wait no longer and, unaware of what was happening outside, stepped through the opening in the wall and stared in amazement at the world of white that awaited him. As he stood there relieving himself in the fresh snow, he felt bitterly cold, colder than he had ever been before in his lifetime. The thought passed through his mind that a person could freeze to death on a night like this. And then he remembered Styles on watch.

When he reached him, the little man was unconscious, covered with two or three inches of powdery snow. Finn at first thought that he was dead. His shouts and entreaties invoked no response. Only the faint trail of icy breath emanating from his nostrils, barely visible, told Finn that a glimmer of life still existed within Style's frozen body. When he gathered Styles into his arms to bring him back to the indentation in the cliff,

the man's lifeless body remained frozen in the grotesque pos-
ture in which Finn had found him. With his unseeing eyes and
whitish-blue flesh, Styles was clearly not far from death.

Kerrivan and the others, still asleep inside the indentation,
were unaware of the drama unfolding around them until Finn
shouted them awake, and laid the lifeless body of Styles on the
ground before them. Then for the first time since they had
arrived there on the mountain, Finn took charge. Within the
matter of a few minutes he had a small fire going on the floor
of the indentation, something that the men rarely did because
the smoke from an inside fire usually tended to blind and choke
them, and gathered all of the bedding that had only minutes
earlier covered the other sleeping men. After wrapping Style's
body in several layers of cloth, he placed him next to the fire
and began to rub his frozen face and extremities.

When, after several minutes, there was still no further sign
of life or apparent improvement in Style's condition, Kerrivan
and the Shannahan brothers knew that the man's departure
was imminent. Finn, however, wasn't ready to give up. He
didn't like Styles. He hated him in fact, but accepted in his own
enigmatic psyche that the evil little man lying on the ground in
front of him was nevertheless human, like himself, and had
suffered the same hardships and deprivations as he, Kerrivan
and the Shannahan brothers had. Knowing nothing better to
do, he simply sat down on the ground next to him, gathered his
wrapped body into the bulk of his own massive frame, and held
him there, willing him back to life as he did so.

He remained there a long time holding Styles, the Snitch,
the man he despised, in his arms like a baby while Kerrivan
and the Shannahan brothers watched in skeptical silence. The
snow continued to fall softly outside, but the rising
morning sun had by this time already driven the outside
temperature up a degree or two.

Finally, after what seemed like an eternity, Finn felt the
slight tremor of Style's body against his own. A few minutes
later the little man gave a soft sigh, opened his eyes briefly,
smiled weakly at Finn, and immediately fell back to sleep
again. Blood flowed once more in his frozen veins, and he was
out of danger. Only the permanent frost damage to a few of his

fingers and toes would later remind Styles that he had come within a hair's breadth of losing his life, and that only the caring and persistence of the man who had once tried to beat him into oblivion had saved him.

The second significant event of that year occurred about three weeks later in the early days of December, long after the premature November snow had melted and disappeared into the ground. Kerrivan himself was on watch when his attention was drawn to a solitary figure making its way toward the mountain waving what appeared to be a large white flag. When the man came close enough to be seen more clearly, Kerrivan could ascertain that he also carried with him a bundle of some sort, and was dressed in a black garment that Kerrivan took to be a priest's cassock. He decided he would wait a little longer before alerting the others.

The approaching man stopped his advance about a quarter of a mile short of the mountain, and remained there walking around within a small section of the open wilderness for a long period of time. His gesticulations, which alternated between flag-waving, hoisting the bundle over his head, and gesturing back toward the coast, were obviously designed to attract the attention of someone on the mountain, no doubt Kerrivan himself and the other members of his band.

When the man finally left, after what Kerrivan judged to be at least an hour, Kerrivan was so intrigued by what he had witnessed that he left his post without telling the others and trailed after the departing figure, being very careful to maintain a safe distance and making sure that he himself wasn't seen. He had deduced that the man's attempt to communicate with him had been so simplistic and so blatantly open that it was highly unlikely to be a ruse to entice him into some sort of trap.

When the man reached the edge of the woods, Kerrivan saw him place his bundle up into the branches of the large oak tree in which he, Finn, and Styles had hidden earlier, and then disappear into the woods, obviously on his way back to Renews.

When Kerrivan retrieved the bundle from the tree, having first waited long enough to assure himself that there was nobody else around, and examined its contents, he knew that he and his companions had at least one friend in the area. The ritual that took place that day would be repeated many times over the next two years. On a regular basis, about once a month, the priest would come close enough to the mountain to make himself visible, retreat and leave a package in the tree, and then go back where he had come from.

The outlaws would soon come to realize that their benefactor was concerned not only for their earthly comforts, but also for their spiritual well-being, for some of his subsequent packages of kindness included a set of rosary beads, a small metal crucifix, and a number of other items of a parochial nature meant to reach their souls, in addition to the tea, bread, potatoes, dried fish, and items of clothing for their mouths and bodies.

fourteen

Father Fabian O'Donnell was a relative newcomer to the settlement of Renews. Having arrived in the small fishing community only a few weeks before the *Fortress* made its appearance, he had been among the crowd on the beach that morning several months earlier when Captain Smith had assembled the people of Renews to question them about the disappearance of the three men who had escaped from his custody.

Tall and painfully thin, the young priest had been born twenty-five years earlier. He was the fifth son of Michael O'Donnell, a tenant farmer who, along with his wife, Mary, managed a ten acre parcel of land in the village of Claras Graen in County Cork, Ireland, for an absentee English landlord whom they rarely saw. The large O'Donnell family was typical of most families throughout Ireland at the time, and included an equal number of girls, ten children in all. Two others had died in infancy. Fabian was the youngest.

The family survived from year to year on a small corner of this section of land that they managed, not much more than a half acre, on which O'Donnell was permitted to grow a few vegetables to feed himself, his wife and his ten children, and to keep a pig or two. Everything else went to the landlord in England. The proceeds from his parcel of land in Claras Graen and a number of others that he owned in Ireland maintained the landlord in a life of luxury in London that the poor Irish men, women and children who worked his farms could not even imagine.

From the very beginning, it was obvious to the rest of the family that Fabian was different from them. From the time he was old enough to develop some understanding of the world into which he had been born, his brothers and sisters, who continually quarreled and fought with each other and with the other children of the village, usually left him alone to play and to do his assigned childhood chores in peace. They had already sensed in him the extreme natural warmth, kindness, and gentle spirit that, as time went on, increasingly manifested itself in his speech, manner, and actions.

Despite his gentle nature and obvious inclination toward the more intellectual side of life, perhaps engendered and encouraged by his mother who told him unending tales of Ireland and its storied past, he was not lazy or idle. He did his fair share of the hard physical work that had to be done on the farm every day and often volunteered to help his brothers and sisters when his own chores were completed.

Fabian was not much more than a toddler when his mother had one day declared, "Thanks be to God. I finally got a priest in the family after rearing nine farmers."

And, indeed, Fabian O'Donnell was born to be a man of God. Everyone knew it. He knew it himself, and as he grew older he began to look forward to the day when his entry into the ecclesiastical world of the priesthood would become a reality.

Finally, one morning shortly after Fabian's twelfth birthday, Michael O'Donnell dressed both himself and his youngest son in their best clothes, which were not much even by poor Irish standards, and made the two day journey by foot to the town of Waterford in the adjoining Waterford County. There he hoped to get an audience with Bishop O'Toole, who was the elder statesman of the Roman Catholic Church in the County as well as the head of the seminary where young men trained for the priesthood. Armed with a letter of recommendation from Father Murphy, the local priest of Claras Graen who had known the boy from birth, the father and son had to wait another two days before they were finally successful in obtaining the audience that they sought.

The interview lasted nearly forty minutes, much longer than O'Donnell had expected or dared to hope for, during which the boy was quizzed and grilled until he thought that his head would surely burst. The old Bishop agreed to keep the boy at the seminary for a period of three months, after which he would make a final decision on the boy's suitability for the priesthood. While the boy's knowledge of worldly and ecclesiastical matters often fell well short of the mark during the interview, Bishop O'Toole had immediately recognized the same qualities of character in the boy that Fabian's own family and many others in Claras Graen had already observed.

When Michael O'Donnell returned to Waterford three months later, he went back home the next day alone, and Fabian, his youngest son, would never again in his lifetime do another day's work on the section of land in Claras Graen. Except for the one visit that he was permitted to make each year to see his parents and his brothers and sisters, usually in September, Fabian would spend the next twelve years of his life in Ireland at the seminary in Waterford. First as a student learning literature, geography, mathematics, history, and the various other subjects that would comprise his basic education as well as his religious training. Then as an acolyte or priest in training, and his final three years as a curate assisting the Bishop and the other priests in the conduct of their activities within the Seminary and the parish that it served.

Then one day, when he was still a few months short of his twenty-fifth birthday, Fabian was informed by Bishop O'Toole, who had taken a great liking to the young man from Claras Graen, that he was being sent to do God's work in a small parish in Newfoundland. The only knowledge that Fabian, now Father Fabian, had of the large island two thousand miles away was a brief reference to it in one of the textbooks he had studied as a student. The parish of Renews, which he was told included the settlements of Fermeuse, Aquaforte, Cappahayden and Renews Proper, was a place he had never even heard of before, but which would now become his new home.

Before leaving for Newfoundland, he made one last visit home. This time, when he looked around him, he suddenly saw the section of land in Claras Graen and the work that his family did there in a new light, and he marveled at the miracle that his mother and father had achieved in raising a large family of healthy, robust children on such a tiny piece of ground.

His father, now sixty-seven, was still hale and hearty and enjoyed his pipe and a pint or two at the end of each day as much as he ever had. The health of his mother, who was now also past her sixtieth birthday, however, had gradually deteriorated during her youngest son's extended stay in Waterford. Her once strong body that had done a full day's work the equal of any man, was now only capable of sitting at the kitchen table or outside on the doorstep while her daughters did most of the household chores and tasks that she had always done herself.

When Fabian shook his father's and his brothers' hands, kissed his mother and his sisters goodbye, and caught the cart that would take him back to the Seminary in Waterford, the thought crossed his mind that he might never see any of them again. And, indeed, he wouldn't.

Although he had spent his entire life on an island surrounded by the sea, he had only seen the ocean a few times and had never before actually ventured out on it. The short voyage to Liverpool, England, where he would board the much larger ship that would take him to Newfoundland, was a revelation. He was exhilarated and fascinated by the gentle movement of the vessel as she slipped quietly through the waves, the feel and smell of the salty air, the slapping of the ship's canvas sails, and the constant creaking and groaning of her riggings. He had also found immense pleasure and enjoyment in the camaraderie of the other passengers traveling on the ship with him.

His voyage across the Atlantic, however, was an entirely different matter. From the moment the ship met the first high rolling seas and winds that would buffet and batter her for most of the two thousand mile voyage, he had experienced continuing bouts of seasickness that simply would not pass. The mutual efforts of himself and other equally sick passengers to help each other did little to ease either his or their discomfort. Time and time again the overwhelming stench of vomit, urine, and human waste drove him up on deck, where he would remain until the biting winds and freezing spray forced him down again. He could scarcely look at the meager allowance of food that was offered to him, let alone eat it. The only thing he could manage was an occasional cup of hot tea and a bite or two of ship biscuit. By the time he finally arrived in the Plantation of Ferryland eighteen days later, he had shed ten or twelve pounds that his slender frame could ill afford to lose.

His first night in Newfoundland, because of the lateness of

the hour of his arrival, was spent on the ship in Ferryland Harbour. At dawn the next morning he set out on the eight-mile trek to the settlement of Renews, passing through the communities of Aquaforte and Fermeuse along the way. The large sack that he carried on his back held all of his worldly possessions – his clerical vestments, some old clothes, his other set of underwear and socks, a bible, and a small piece of cheese and half a loaf of bread that he had been given by the vessel's sympathetic cook, along with a letter of introduction that he was to give to the current priest in residence. By the time he reached his destination, he knew that he had stepped into a strange new world. Renews and the other settlements that he had seen were in some respects a bit like the Ireland that he had known from childhood. The many different shades of green of the surrounding countryside and the speech of the people he met along the way were familiar to him, although he sometimes had to listen carefully to catch the gist of some sentence spoken in the unique local dialect of the area or to ask the meaning of some word or phrase that he had never heard before.

Yet, at the same time, his new surroundings were vastly different. The open sea and the rugged coast on which the small settlements clung were nothing like the rolling green farmlands he had known in Ireland. The ever-present smell of manure and the pungent odor of burning peat that had permeated the air of Claras Graen were now replaced with the smell of spruce wood-fires burning in the stoves and fireplaces of the community, the briny air blowing in from the ocean, and the smell of fish drying on the beaches and on the high bough-covered platforms that the settlers called "flakes" – or just rotting on the small vegetable gardens that he saw everywhere.

Father Fabian's arrival in Newfoundland could not have been more timely if he had himself been able to plan it to the last detail. He had been sent over from Ireland to assist the aging and ailing Father Connolly, who had written his superiors in Waterford a year earlier informing them of his failing health and suggesting that they consider sending someone to replace him as the head of the Parish of Renews before too many more years passed. Father Connolly, now well into his late seventies, had served the parish of Renews in an official capacity for the last ten years and, before that, as one of the unofficial "roving" priests whose presence in Newfoundland had until then been prohibited by law. Subject to reprisal and severe punishment if they were caught, he and a few other priests like him had served the Roman Catholic population of the Southern Shore of the Avalon Peninsula and other areas of Newfoundland in secret for many years, shielded and protected from the Protestant authorities by the Roman Catholic men and women whose souls and spiritual well-being they attended.

For, only three weeks after Father Fabian's arrival, Father Connolly died. One morning when Fabian climbed the stairs to bring the ailing old priest his morning tea, he had found him staring vacantly at the ceiling, his flesh ice-cold to the touch, and his mouth and the left side of his face drawn in a grotesque grin by the stroke that had taken him away sometime during the night.

Fabian obeyed his first instinct and closed the old man's sightless eyes and folded his hands and arms across his chest. Having then covered him with a blanket, he administered the last rites, the first time he had ever done so himself although he had been present on many other occasions when other more senior priests had performed the sacred ritual. After that he simply sat for a very long time in the only chair in the large, drafty bedroom in which the old priest had passed away, and wondered what he should do next. In the brief time that Fabian had been in Renews, Father Connolly had been too sick to instruct him in any way in his duties and responsibilities. Indeed, there were times when Fabian wondered if the old man had even been aware of his presence in the Presbytery at all.

Finally, after a long period of inaction, the young priest asserted himself enough to meet with some of the settlers, introduce himself, and see to it that Father Connolly was properly waked and buried. After doing so, he wrote a dispatch to Bishop O'Toole in Waterford informing him of Father Connolly's death and requesting further instructions, knowing that it might take upwards of another year before he received a reply.

And then the full realization hit him that he was now, still two months shy of twenty-five, the spiritual head of the four settlements that comprised the Parish of Renews, and the father-confessor to the more than one thousand men, women and children who lived there.

For the first time in his life, he was lost and afraid. From the days of his earliest childhood in Claras Graen and through his entire stay at the seminary in Waterford, he had lived a structured and ordered life in which somebody else, always someone with authority over him, had instructed and guided him in the tasks and duties that he had to perform. He had never really been required to think and act on his own, or ever been given any significant personal responsibility of any kind. And now he was alone in a strange new land, with no one to turn to for the help and guidance that he needed more than at any other time in his life. In despair and panic, he wanted to return to Ferryland and catch the next boat back to Ireland. But he knew that he couldn't.

What he did do, however, was something that he had done all his life. He prayed. He prayed longer and more earnestly than ever before until he finally fell asleep, still on his knees, imploring the God that had always seen him through before to help him again now in his time of distress. That night, for the first time in more than a week, he slept soundly without dreaming or waking at all. In the morning he awoke refreshed, renewed and imbued with the energy and determination to go forth to do the work that he had been sent to perform.

He held morning and evening mass in the tiny Church situated on the north side of the harbor. It was so small that the first time he saw it, his initial thought had been that it could probably fit in the porch of the one he had served in Waterford. He heard confession, he christened new babies and buried the dead, married couples, and visited the aged, the sick, and the infirm of the settlements of Renews, Fermeuse, Aquaforte, and Cappahayden. He also familiarized himself with the administrative and financial matters of the parish. Not being quite sure if any of his responsibilities extended as far north as the Ferryland Plantation, he journeyed there one day after he had made his presence known to almost every family in the other four settlements. On his arrival there, however, he found that the Ferryland Plantation had not one, but two priests of their own and that Ferryland was the beginning of a separate and much larger parish that extended northward along the Southern Shore as far as the settlement of Bay Bulls, a distance of some thirty miles.

Thus, in the weeks and months following his own arrival and the death of Father Connolly, he discovered for himself the full scope and boundaries of his parish, and had grown steadily, with confidence and the guiding hand of God, into his full role as a priest.

The people of the parish quickly came to like their new young priest, and then to love and admire him. Unlike the grizzled old Father Connolly, who had ruled their souls with an iron hand, utilizing fear and intimidation as much as he did the teachings of the Bible, Father Fabian came to them with a quiet dignity and humility, spreading warmth and sunshine wherever he went. He found time to speak to everybody, from the youngest to the oldest, and brought the men and women of the parish comfort and solace in their times of need.

And, indeed, he could have done no less. For the young priest who moved among them, who had scarcely had a cross moment or an evil thought in his lifetime, was truly a man of God.

As the priest-in-residence of the parish, Father Fabian received two privileges besides his small income. He was permitted to live in the two-story frame house in Renews that served as the Presbytery and official center of business for the Roman Catholic parish. As was the custom in most other Roman Catholic parishes along the Shore, the Parish of Renews also stocked the Presbytery with an ample supply of firewood in the form of a stack of logs to ensure that the priest-in-residence could keep himself from freezing to death during the cold fall and winter months of Newfoundland.

The generosity of the Parish of Renews did not, however, as it did in some other larger and more prosperous settlements, extend to the provision of domestic help in any form. Father Fabian was expected to look after his own personal care, and, in between his priestly duties, find the time to do his own housework, wash his clothes and bedding, fetch drinking water, chop splits and junks for the fire, and attend to all of the other details that went with the management and upkeep of a residence. And, although he was occasionally given a loaf of bread or a fish or two by someone in the parish, he was also expected to feed himself out of the pittance that he was paid for his work.

For the first six or seven weeks of his stay in the Presbytery, Father Fabian slept on a cot in the small guest bedroom that sometimes also served to wake some person who had died in the parish. He could not yet quite bring himself to sleep in the big four-poster bed in the larger bedroom in which he had found Father Connolly that morning almost six months earlier. Then, when an elderly impoverished man of the settlement passed quietly away in his sleep one night and the spare room in the Presbytery was needed for his wake, Father Fabian, left with no other alternative, finally moved into the larger bedroom.

Before doing so, he carefully packed most of the old priest's few personal possessions away in the battered trunk that the old man had kept under his bed, keeping aside only a few things that he thought might be of better use to someone else. These included a handful of ancient, dog-eared books which he moved downstairs to the kitchen where anyone who was interested, including himself, might read them at their leisure. He thought that the old man's robes might come in handy for himself at some later date as the few priest's garments that he had brought with him from Ireland could not be expected to last indefinitely. He also kept aside the thick woolen blanket that had been partially covering the old man's body when he had found him dead in his bed. It now seemed so long ago. He made a mental note to himself to remember to give it to some poor soul who might benefit from it most.

One evening in late September Father Fabian sat alone enjoying his meal of fresh fish stew and tea which he had just prepared. It was almost six months to the day since his arrival in Newfoundland the previous spring. He was trying, as he ate, to think of an appropriate topic for his next sermon when he heard the knock on his door that would, although he didn't have any way of realizing it at the time, change his life and affect him in a deeply profound and sad but, in the end, uplifting way.

He recognized the man at his door as one whom he had met during his earlier visitations around Renews. He knew the man's first name was Patrick, but couldn't at that moment recall his surname.

"Hello, Patrick. What brings you knocking on my door on this fine evening?"

"Well, Father, I've come to tell you to be locking your door at night and to be looking after yourself. There's a lot of thievery going on in Renews these days. Same thing up in Fermeuse, and even down in Cappahayden. 'Tis them wild men out there in the barrens, you know, the ones who escaped from the ship. Everyone says they're still out there, and it's them that's doing the stealing. Sure the poor women and the children are almost frightened out of their wits."

"Thank you for coming to tell me that, Patrick. Now would you like to join me in a drop of tea before you go?"

The man, having delivered the message that he felt was his personal obligation to the young priest and perhaps feeling a little bit uncomfortable being alone in the presence of a man of the cloth, declined.

"No thanks, Father, I'll just be on my way now. But remember what I told you, won't you?"

When he departed, the young priest returned to his meal and the matter of his sermon. He thought briefly about what the man had just told him. He himself had heard the rumors about the supposedly nearby outlaws during his movement around the parish, but had not given the matter any serious thought. Nor, despite Patrick's warning, did he do so now, for within a minute or two he was again immersed in his thoughts about what he wanted to say in his next sermon to the people. That night, as he had done on all previous nights and would continue to do for all of his remaining nights in the Presbytery, he neglected or forgot to lock his door.

October brought with it a considerable drop in temperature and Father Fabian, for the first time since moving into the Presbytery, turned his serious attention to the woodpile. Until now, whenever he had needed fuel for cooking his food and boiling his water, he had simply rummaged in the nearby fields and copses for dead-fall branches and alders, twigs, leaves or bits of discarded wood or timber. But everyone in the parish had warned him about the severity of Newfoundland winters, and he knew that he would soon have to begin to get in a proper supply of firewood for the coming winter months.

Whenever he could spare an hour or two from his other work and duties, he would don the pair of much mended and patched trousers and old flannel shirt that he had brought over with him from Ireland, and attack the large stack of logs that the parish had provided. The first two or three sessions with the ax had left his frail body aching and sore. He was not used to any form of physical labour except the endless miles he trod to carry out his work in the parish. But invariably, by the end of each session, several logs from the pile were reduced to sixteen-inch junks that would be used to feed the three fireplaces of the Presbytery. Once his arms and shoulders became accustomed to the hard work, he actually began to enjoy and look forward to the work sessions, sometimes stripping to the waist, taking pleasure from the feel of sweat and the cool autumn air on his back as he swung the axe.

As the days of October went by, the stack of logs grew slowly smaller and the junk-pile steadily grew larger and higher. By the end of the month, he had a good-sized pile of junks ready to be stored inside, but he knew that it would have to grow much larger still if it were to see him warmly through the winter.

The early days of November were a little colder, although on most nights Father Fabian still left the fireplaces unlit and slept comfortably snuggled under the warmth of the single thick blanket that covered his bed. The vegetable crops of the settlement had all been harvested, and several of the settlers had thought fit to bring him small gifts of potatoes, turnips, cabbages and carrots, all of which were now safely stored in his larder and would hopefully see him well-fed for many weeks, perhaps until Christmas.

And then one morning in the second week of November, he awoke, freezing, to a world of white. The surfaces of the water in his wash basin and drinking bucket had frozen over during the night, and the four inches of snow that had fallen silently and steadily during the night covered the grounds of the Presbytery, the settlement of Renews, and the surrounding hills and barrens for as far as he could see.

Father Fabian had seen snow before during his childhood years in Ireland, but rarely and only in the deeper months of winter. Even then it was usually only a light dusting that disappeared again within a day or two. The sight of ankle-deep snow in early November was a spectacle he had never encountered before. Now he became concerned that perhaps he had left the cutting of his firewood a bit late after all.

Bishop O'Toole and the other priests of the Seminary in Waterford had warned him before he left for Newfoundland that the winters he would encounter there would be cold and long. This early onset of frost and snow in Renews, however, was an anomaly. While it is true that the winters along the Southern Shore of the Avalon Peninsula are indeed harsher than those of Ireland, the winter climate of this stretch of coastline, due to its proximity to the ocean, is considered to be mild in comparison to most other areas of Newfoundland. In most years, real winter does not set in on the Shore until late December or early January, and the average annual accumulation of snowfall there rarely exceeds a dozen inches or so for the entire winter period, far less than the amount of snow received in most of the more northerly parts of the island and its interior.

By the next morning, the temperature had again risen to its normal autumn level and the snow disappeared as quickly as it had arrived. The only evidence that it had fallen at all was the glistening pools of water everywhere and the odd patch of slush in some shaded area that the sun couldn't quite reach. Father Fabian was relieved and promised himself that he would make a concerted effort to get his wood-chopping completed within the next week or two.

When he next returned to the chopping block, however, again clad in his patched trousers and shirt that by now were in dire need of a good washing, he couldn't find his axe. After a quick search of the grounds of the Presbytery and after checking inside, the ax was still nowhere to be seen. He was certain that he had left it where he always did, embedded in the end of the large juniper chopping block where it would be readily available when he needed it again. He even checked with the men and women who lived in some of the nearby houses to see if they knew anything about it, but to no avail.

The loss of the axe was a serious matter. Without it, he would never be able to stockpile enough junks to last him through the winter months. Fortunately, his predicament was soon solved for him by a neighbor who readily offered to share an axe with him so that he could continue his work, and he was able to get his junk-pile finished on schedule.

Although he still kept an eye out for the axe whenever he was outdoors around the Presbytery, he didn't give the matter much further thought until a week later when a wooden water-pail that he had set outside to catch rainwater falling from the Presbytery roof, which people told him was much better than groundwater for his laundry, mysteriously disappeared. Then, for the first time, he began to wonder if the stories and rumors about the wild men from the barrens might indeed be true. And then in the first week of December, the pair of long-legged fleece underwear that he had brought with him from Waterford at the insistence of Bishop O'Toole, who told him he would surely need them in his new environment, went missing from the bushes upon which he had laid them along with the rest of his washing to dry. He now became convinced in his own mind that the existence of the outlaws was a reality.

Even after these injustices had been committed against him, Father Fabian's kind and gentle nature would only permit him to think about the outlaws in terms of the suffering and deprivation that they must feel living out there in the wilderness. Unlike Father Fabian, however, the other people of the parish only thought of the outlaws as renegade criminals, robbers, pillagers of their settlements, cruel and brutal men capable of the most heinous actions imaginable against their wives and children.

And the longer Father Fabian thought about these wretched souls reduced to a life in hiding and scavenging for their survival, the more compassion and sympathy he felt for their plight. He knew in his heart, in a way that few other men could, that these poor men, whoever they were, must feel pain and hunger like everybody else, experience the same emotions, and feel the need for companionship and human kindness. They had surely all once been boys like himself, who had wanted only to play, laugh, and sing, and to run freely with the feel of the soft grass on their feet. They were still God's creations, and whatever his crime, not a single man among them was beyond redemption.

As Christmas neared, Father Fabian's thoughts became so preoccupied with the wild men on the barrens that he had difficulty keeping his attention firmly focused on anything else. And he came to the conclusion that he would like to meet them face to face to try to help them in some way if he could. He surmised, like most other people in the parish, that the outlaws must have their hideout somewhere on or near the Butterpot mountain, as that was the only place on the wild, open barrens that could offer the shelter that they needed and provide an unobstructed view of anyone approaching from the settlements. Still, he knew that they would never knowingly let him come near, or reveal themselves to him, or to anyone else for that matter.

Father Fabian's dilemma remained unsolved until one day when he was visiting an elderly couple in Fermeuse and heard the story of the Fairy Tree. It was then that he came up with the idea that he hoped might eventually bring him in contact with the men on the barrens.

The Fairy Tree was unique, undoubtedly the only one of its kind on the entire Southern Shore. Surrounded by the smaller species of spruce, fir, and juniper trees that dominated the sparse forest areas of the region and shared the acid soil of the area with it, the Fairy Tree was a giant oak tree that had somehow grown to gargantuan proportions, dwarfing everything around it. The girth of the magnificent tree was the equal of its height, and its branches spread so wide and so densely that no grass or vegetation other than damp, springy moss could grow in the seventy-five diameter cast of their shadow.

The origin of the tree was a mystery. Undoubtedly it was a fluke of nature for it grew there in an area where no other oak trees existed. How it had gotten there without the benefit of an acorn from some other nearby tree of the same species was a question that defied answer. Perhaps some settler had planted it there in that unlikely spot many years earlier. Or perhaps a bird flying past overhead had dropped an acorn that had somehow taken root. Even if that were the case, the conception of the tree would still have been a miracle for even in the more charitable climate and soil conditions of countries like England or France only one acorn in thousands ever eventually ever produced a tree. The odds against a single random acorn taking root in the inhospitable wilderness of the Southern Shore would have been astronomical.

Yet, whatever it's origin, the existence of the tree was a fact of life. It was perhaps an even greater miracle that no one had yet cut it down for the vast amount of valuable hardwood that its massive trunk and huge branches would yield. Maybe the people of the area were afraid to do so, for the tree had a mystical history of its own.

Many years earlier, a man from Fermeuse whom someone had nicknamed Friar Tuck because of his portly frame and monkish appearance, but whose real name nobody could remember, claimed that he had been bewitched by fairies while he rested and slept under the tree after an afternoon of berry picking on the barrens. When he awoke he found himself surrounded by fairies and gnomes who danced and pranced around him as he lay there unable to move. They kept him, so he claimed, prisoner for three days. When he finally returned to the settlement and told his story, most people scoffed and only a few, if any, gave it a second thought at the time.

A week later, however, when his lifeless body was discovered on the beach of Fermeuse, the people of Fermeuse and the other settlements in the area knew that Friar Tuck had not lied after all. For anyone who had ever listened to the countless Irish stories of fairies, elves and gnomes knew that any man or woman who saw these creatures in their place of residence and then disclosed their whereabouts to others, would die a quick and merciless death. There were no marks anywhere on Tuck's body to indicate how he had died, and his small fishing boat drifted aimlessly by itself a short distance from the shore. But to the people of the parish of Renews, there was no doubt in their minds why he had died, and who had killed him.

Thus, the tale of Friar Tuck and the Fairy Tree passed into legend. And the Irish people of this part of the Southern Shore, whose country of origin was the ancestral home of fairies everywhere, now had a few "little people" of their very own to brag about.

Father Fabian's plan was simple. Without telling anyone else, he packed some bread and a few vegetables, along with an item or two of old clothing and a large white sheet, into a sack and set off through the mile-and-a-half thick patch of forest at whose western edge the Butterpot barrens began, toward the spot where he hoped to find the massive tree. Although he had never seen it before, he had a good idea where to find it.

No one witnessed his passage through the woods except the reclusive woman who lived alone in the hut in the clearing, although he himself hadn't observed her when he passed through. When he arrived at his destination and found the Fairy Tree exactly where he expected it to be, he walked out onto the barrens until he judged that he was within seeing distance of anyone who might be watching from the mountain. He attached the white sheet that he had brought with him to a long, thin sapling that he had picked up along the way, and began to wave it toward the mountain.

He remained there for almost an hour, pacing back and forth with the sack in his hand, waving the white sheet continuously as he willed the men to see him from the distance. When he finally returned to the Fairy Tree, he placed the sack in the crook of two of its branches, high enough so that it would not be readily seen by anyone who might venture past.

He then left again for the Presbytery, hoping that the outlaws, if they were really out there, had seen him, and would, after he had gone, be curious enough to come to see what he placed in the tree.

fifteen

In the small clearing in the woods, set back about a mile from the rest of the settlement, bounded on one side by Peter's Brook, Hannah Martin rested for a few minutes, surveying her day's work. In the twilight of the late October afternoon, with darkness near, she realized that it would take her at least part of the next day, perhaps all of it, to finish her task of enlarging and deepening the hole in the ground in which she planned to cache her recently dug crop of potatoes for the coming winter.

Last winter she had lost the topmost layers to frost and burrowing rodents. And this year, the early November frost that had almost claimed Styles life on the mountain a few short miles away, had almost taken her new crop of potatoes as well. Only her foresight in temporarily covering them with several layers of freshly cut boughs after digging them up had saved them.

She was tired. She was hungry and thirsty. And more than anything else in the world she wanted to go home – to be able to return to the life of comfort and security that she had forsaken three years earlier. She knew, or at least hoped, that she would be welcomed back in an instant if she returned, and that it was only her own foolish pride and the circumstances of her leaving that prevented her from doing so. She was reconciled to the fact that she would undoubtedly spend the remaining days of her life living here alone on the outskirts of Renews, shunned and avoided by the other people of the settlement.

She was tall, much taller than any other woman that she had ever known or met, and the stoop of her shoulders and the forward inclination of her neck and head were perhaps as much the result of an unconscious attempt to make herself as short as other women as they were her own natural physical characteristics. A few wisps of her long black hair matted into the sweat of her brow and her face. The rest, already flecked with gray even though she had only recently reached her thirty-second year, was tied behind her head in a bun.

Her thin, almost gaunt frame betrayed the hunger that she often felt. In a face that most people would have called common, at best, only the intensity of her slate gray eyes and the firm set of her jaw gave any hint of the keen intelligence and indomitable strength of character that lay within.

She had come here from Harbour Grace three years earlier, where she had lived and spent the first twenty-nine years of her life. The mother who had given her birth had sacrificed her own life in the process, and her father, grieved and shocked by the sudden and unexpected loss of his wife, was left with five other small children to raise by himself and was incapable of looking after another. When Hannah was only a day old, he had wrapped her in a warm blanket and walked the length of Harbour Grace to bring her to his only sister with a plea that she look after the infant for him for a short while. Little did his sister know, when she consented, that the newborn baby's short stay would extend into a period of twenty-nine years.

Beatrice Mercer (nee Martin), the aunt who had at first reluctantly agreed to look after the infant but who within the space of a few short weeks had come to so love and cherish it that she began to think of it as her own, was herself childless. Although a widow, she had sufficient means of maintaining herself and Hannah, and made sure that the child was properly cared for, christened, and baptized. She and the baby lived alone in the two-story frame house that her late husband, George, had built on the extreme west end of Water Street, just far enough removed from the main hustle and bustle of the waterfront to give him and Beatrice some degree of quiet and privacy. George, when he died, had left her not only the house, but a large fishing vessel and fishing rooms complete with all manner of fishing gear that, when sold, gave her a nest egg that would see her through her lifetime if she managed it properly.

Aunt Beatrice never shielded Hannah from the fact that she was not her real mother, and Hannah never got to know her father very well because shortly after her birth he remarried and moved to St. John's, eighty miles away. Despite the circumstances of her birth and her early years, Hannah lived a happy and contented childhood, as safe and secure in the custody of Aunt Beatrice as any child could possibly be anywhere.

Aunt Beatrice was an independent woman and had no desire to remarry. She was, unlike most other women of the time, also educated and trained in classical music. On most evenings, after supper dishes had been cleaned and put away, she played the harpsichord that George had brought her from Poole, England. It was one of the few in the community and perhaps in all of Newfoundland. The other great passion of her life was her religion. She was a devout Christian, as staunch a Protestant as ever walked the face of the earth. And she raised Hannah in such a way that she hoped that the child too would in time possess most of these same qualities.

By the time Hannah was nine or ten years old, she could read almost as well as her aunt, who had taught her, and before she reached her fourteenth birthday she had read the Bible in its entirety at least three times. While she openly admitted that she didn't fully understand some of what it said, the more she read the Bible the more its teachings and messages became an integral and important part of her every-day existence. Despite the scarcity of other reading material in the community, she somehow always seemed to find something somewhere to satisfy her unquenchable thirst for news, stories, and information of all kinds. In the absence of anything else, she read and reread the "promise cards" that Aunt Beatrice had placed in strategic locations throughout the house until they were dog-eared and she knew their contents by heart. These were simply boxed-sets of tiny pieces of cardboard measuring about one inch by three inches on which were printed individual verses from the Bible or religious quotations from various other sources. They were meant to be picked at random to give inspiration, guidance, and solace.

Hannah could never remember a time in her life when she hadn't attended church. Every Sunday, and on all other religious days, both she and Aunt Beatrice would dress in their finest clothes, march the quarter of a mile to St. Paul's Anglican Church together regardless of the weather, and seat themselves in their places in the front pew. Their attendance was so regular and so steadfast that the rest of the congregation automatically relinquished these seats to them. Hannah came to know the prayer book, the hymns of the church, and the order of services so well that she could repeat most of them from memory. And Aunt Beatrice took great delight in her prodigy.

Hannah's religious upbringing didn't begin and end with her daily reading of the Bible and her regular attendance in church. Each night before they climbed the stairs to go to bed and each morning when they arose, both she and Aunt Beatrice would kneel together in prayer on the floor of the kitchen and offer thanks for the many blessings that they enjoyed in their tranquil and cozy environment. On many nights, when she herself had finally gotten into her own bed, Hannah would hear her aunt as she continued to pray alone in the adjoining room.

Hannah's peaceful existence, with her reading, and her prayers and her hymns, a comfortable roof over her head, the doting love of Aunt Beatrice, and the friendship of the other girls who lived in this part of Harbour Grace, was almost idyllic. That is, until the summer of her fifteenth year. And then she entered into a time in her life that would bring her much unhappiness and distress, and ultimately great hardship, suffering, and deprivation.

It was during that summer that she, like most other girls of her age, had a growth spurt. Unlike most others, however, who usually shot up an inch or two in the space of a few months and then stopped or leveled off, Hannah's growth spurt didn't stop until, ten months later, she was an even six feet in height. And even then it didn't cease, for within the next year or so she grew another two inches, making her by far the tallest female in the settlement, towering head and shoulders over any other girl or woman, rivaled in height by only a handful of men in all of Conception Bay.

At first pleased with the fact that she was finally growing into a woman, she soon became self-conscious and embarrassed about her appearance as she continued to grow taller and taller. The rest of her body hadn't kept pace with her height, and she took on such a skeletal appearance that her friends and other people began to tease and taunt her. And to make matters worse, her naturally translucent flesh gave her an ethereal look that sometimes shocked people when they first saw her. She began to notice that whenever she walked by, people would often stare at her in a kind of strange fascination, exchange some obvious comment about her, and shake their heads in what could have been a gesture of anything from scorn to pity as she passed.

Her religious upbringing and gentle nature forbade her to lash back and put an early stop to the taunting before it got too far out of hand. And the taunts and the ridiculing continued to grow progressively worse until Hannah, unwilling to endure it any longer, finally stopped associating with the girls whom she had once thought of as her friends. She now kept her own company and seldom strayed very far beyond her own doorstep. Only Aunt Beatrice, who was herself a bit of a loner, had some idea of the torture that her sensitive niece was living, and she became, in addition to being Hannah's mother figure, her best, if not only, real friend and companion.

The years passed slowly for the two reclusive women, and the sting of the earlier hurt and humiliation gradually lessened until Hannah had once again become comfortable and contented with her lot in life. Now when she accompanied Aunt Beatrice on her evening walk, she could manage to smile or say hello to those who had once ridiculed her. She had long since forgiven them in her heart, but she hadn't forgotten the misery they had caused her. Still, she and Aunt Beatrice had everything that they needed to make their lives complete, including each other. And over time, Hannah's once terribly thin body filled out until she was a normal well-proportioned woman, albeit an extremely tall one.

One morning in early June, when Hannah was twenty-nine, she went alone to tend a small vegetable garden that she and Aunt Beatrice maintained in a small clearing on a little knoll about a quarter of a mile from their house. Her purpose was to spread the two pails of caplin that she had gathered from the beach the previous day to compost the carrot, turnip, beet and cabbage seeds that she had planted a few weeks earlier. The main potato garden, the staple of their year-round diet, was much larger and ran adjacent to the house in which they lived.

Aunt Beatrice usually accompanied Hannah whenever she went to the smaller garden, but on this day the older woman stayed behind to finish some sewing that she had started the night before. And it was on that morning, in the small vegetable garden on the knoll, that Hannah saw the smiling face of Ned Madigan for the first time.

The cool morning breeze, which mercifully kept away the black flies and mosquitoes that were always attracted in great swarms by the smell of rotting caplin at this time of year, invigorated her and she felt alert and alive as she spread the caplin over the tiny vegetable shoots that were already beginning to emerge from the ground. So intent was she on her work that she didn't see the man until he spoke to her.

"Now what would a fine colleen like yourself be doin' at a dirty old job like that?"

Startled, at first by the unexpected sound of his voice, and then even more so by the shock of red hair and the grinning face of the man who had suddenly materialized in front of her as if from thin air, she dropped her pail of caplin and her hands flew to her mouth and face. Strangely, for a fleeting moment, despite her shock, she thought that his face was the most beautiful thing she had ever seen. She couldn't speak.

"Ah, now, I didn't mean to be frightening you, girl. I only stopped for a minute to pass the time of day. So I'll just be off on my way again. Top of the mornin' to you."

And as suddenly as he had appeared, he was gone, leaving Hannah in a state of bewilderment and wonder. She wondered who he was and where he had come from. She was sorry now that she hadn't had the presence of mind to have at least said good morning to him. Her first impression was that he was almost as tall as herself, but perhaps not quite. For the rest of the day she was oddly disquieted.

She didn't tell Aunt Beatrice about the strange man in the garden, and tried her best to put him out of her mind. Then, two days later, while she was walking along the Harbour Grace beach in the early morning light looking for more caplin for her vegetable garden, he had suddenly fallen into step beside her and begun to talk to her as if they were old friends.

"Ah, what a fine beautiful morning it is. Sure 'tis a joy to be

alive and kicking on a day like this. Who could ask for more?"

He took the two pails that she carried from her hands and helped her fill them with the tiny fish that were still rolling in great numbers on the beach. He accompanied her back to the garden and helped her spread them around on the ground, talking to her and laughing all the while. She still hadn't spoken to him. Then, as before, he simply said, "Well, I'll be off now," and he was gone again.

By now she was so mystified, if not mesmerized, with the man who had popped into her life so suddenly and with such impact, that she wondered if she would see him again, and began to look forward to his next appearance. She would not be disappointed. For the next morning when she went to fetch water, he was waiting for her at the well.

During the days that followed, she looked everywhere for him, and inevitably, sometime during the day, he would mysteriously appear – never in the presence of Aunt Beatrice or anyone else, but always when Hannah was alone, and then in the most unlikely places and at the oddest of times. He talked to her, told her stories, and made her laugh. Sometimes he even sang to her, strange little songs that she hadn't heard before and whose lines sometimes seemed to make little sense. She conversed openly with him now, and told him all about herself and her life in Harbour Grace. And although she wasn't sure why, she still kept him a secret from Aunt Beatrice.

Then one day in late June, after she had seen him at least a dozen more times, he told her, "Hannah, I'm going away again now for a while. But I'll be back around the end of September, and when I do I want you to come away with me to Renews. I got a fine little cottage there, and I promise you I'll make you happier than the Queen of England. Just be ready when I get here."

And he left. Hannah was so devastated by his departure that she could scarcely muddle through the days that followed. Ned Madigan filled her thoughts night and day. When Aunt Beatrice asked her on several occasions if something was wrong, she couldn't give the woman a truthful answer.

The days and weeks of summer crept pass with agonizing slowness. Time should have lessened her obsession with

Madigan, but it didn't. If anything, it made it worse. No matter how hard she tried to apply herself to other things, she could not shake the image of him from her mind. He even invaded her prayers, and when he did she prayed all the longer and more earnestly with the guilt of it. She knew that she could never go away with him and leave Aunt Beatrice and her home here in Harbour Grace. But all she wanted was to see his smiling face again and to hear the magic of his voice one more time. For like Friar Tuck under the Fairy Tree, she too had been bewitched, not by fairies or elves, but by the tall lanky man with the mass of red hair and the lopsided grin.

And, despite her resolve to the contrary, when Ned Madigan came back as promised in late September, she went away with him. They stole away in the darkness of the night while Aunt Beatrice and the rest of the settlement slept. Unable to tell Aunt Beatrice face to face what she was about to do, she had instead left a note begging her aunt's understanding and forgiveness, knowing full well that the woman who had raised her from infancy and who loved her as dearly as any mother could possibly love a child of her own, would be crushed by her leaving.

Her first misgiving came shortly after they had come ashore in Renews and begun their walk to Ned's cottage on the outskirts of the community. None of the people that they passed along the way had offered any form of greeting or acknowledgment. In fact, Hannah was certain that some of the men and women that they passed had glared at her and Ned with open hostility. When she asked him what was happening, Ned had merely grunted and told her, "Never mind them. Just keep walking, we still got a long way to go."

When they had passed through the settlement and reached the place where Peter's Brook empties into the Renews Harbor, they picked up a well-trodden footpath that followed the meandering course of the river as it flowed through the woods ahead of them. He told her that it would lead them to his cottage in the clearing.

The walk through the woods took much longer than Hannah had expected. Then, when they finally reached the clearing and she saw her new home for the first time, she was devastated. For the nice little cottage that Ned had promised her was nothing more than a hovel, a crudely constructed one-room structure that was generally known throughout Newfoundland at the time as a "leaning tilt." Its sides were made of vertical unpeeled logs, all leaning slightly inward to rest against a rough frame, while the roof simply consisted of similar logs placed lengthwise across the width of the structure, and covered with layers of boughs and moss to keep out the rain and snow. There was no window, and light could only find its way inside through the small square hole in the center of the roof whose purpose, in the absence of a proper chimney, was to allow smoke from an inside wood-fire to escape. The interior, if possible, was even worse. When her eyes became accustomed to the dim light inside, she saw only years of accumulated dirt and filth. She was so shocked that she could scarcely fathom what she saw.

"Surely this is not where we are going to live, is it? It's hardly fit for animals. Why didn't you tell me?" Hot tears stung her face, and she knew she was on the verge of breaking down completely.

"'Tis good enough for you and me, Hannah. There's lots of women around here that would love to have a place like this. And a man, too. That's what's wrong with you, girl, you've never had a man before. But don't worry, you'll soon get used to it."

The mocking in his eyes hurt her even more. She knew that to say anything further would only make the terrible moment even worse.

That night, as she lay unwillingly beside the man who had brought her there, the full horror of what she had done finally sunk in. Ned, who snored blissfully next to her on the dirty, bough covered bench, had never once mentioned marriage. She had automatically assumed it. She now wanted only to escape and, knowing nothing else to do, cried softly to herself until the first rays of daylight finally filtered in through the smoke hole in the roof, never once having closed her eyes in sleep during that entire period of time.

In her heart she knew that she had made a terrible mistake. And when Ned told her, "Hannah, I'll be having my breakfast now," she suddenly saw him as an entirely different man from the one she had known back in Harbour Grace.

And, in truth, he was. He was, in reality, a grand deceiver who over a period of years had robbed and swindled a great number of people in the four settlements that comprised the Parish of Renews. He had done it so subtly and with such finesse that the people he had conned had not realized it until long afterward. There was never enough evidence to enable anyone to bring the force of the law against him, and he continued to live among them year after year with impunity, unbelievably still finding new ways to rob them of their possessions.

More galling still was the fact that every week when the people of the parish gathered in the church for Sunday mass, Madigan would wait until they were all assembled and seated before making his own entrance. He would then strut in absolute arrogance to the front pew, in full view of everyone present, daring them to confront him in the sanctuary of the church, rubbing their noses in the fact that they couldn't touch him. On the one occasion that he had forced Hannah go with him, she had felt as affronted by the strange Roman Catholic service, so different from her own, as she had been humiliated and ashamed to be at Madigan's side. Still, she noted that although the priest conducting mass seemed very old and frail, his thunderous voice and intense glare had the congregation hanging onto his every word.

The settlers hated Madigan with great passion. And now, some of their hatred and hostility, although she hadn't realized it at first, was transferred to Hannah herself by association. And when, after a short time, they found out that she wasn't even married to Madigan but simply living in sin with him, their hostility towards her heightened even more. And finally, when they discovered that she was a Protestant, one of the great Newfoundland majority that had harassed and persecuted Roman Catholic settlers since the early days of the Colony of Avalon, their animosity toward her knew no bounds.

Trapped in a snare of her own making, she didn't know what to do or where to turn for help and guidance. Finally, unable to endure another night in the filthy conditions of the hovel, she began to clean it up. If she had to stay there, at least she would try to give it some semblance of cleanliness and order. She swept the earthen floor to rid it of the dirt and debris that had lain there for years. Then she did the same with the walls. She removed the dirty boughs, many of which were blasty and reduced to nothing more than needles, from the sleeping bench and replaced them with new fresh ones from the surrounding woods. She left the door, which was nothing more than a few animal hides stitched together, opened constantly so that the fresh air entering the hovel could dissipate the stench inside. She even persuaded Ned to cut a small opening in one of the walls to let more light and air enter.

When she had finished with the cleaning of the interior of the leaning tilt, she turned her attention outdoors. She attacked the potato garden that was so over-run with weeds and grass that it was a wonder that the few paltry potatoes that grew there could survive at all. She stacked wood, and fetched fresh drinking water from the brook that flowed pass about a hundred yards away.

And by doing all these things, she was sometimes able to blot the horror of her new existence from her mind for a few minutes. All the while, she prayed and asked God for guidance and forgiveness. She would not let herself dwell too much on the life she had left behind, because to do so would surely have pushed her to the brink of insanity.

Oddly, Ned had felt irked and annoyed by the improvements Hannah had made to their environment, and he took advantage of every opportunity to ridicule and taunt her. Still, to his credit he never once hit her or threatened her with physical harm. About a month after their arrival in Renews, he announced to her one morning that he was leaving for a while. He said he was going to St. John's and didn't know when he would be back, but to expect him by Christmas.

She realized now that what she had thought was love for Madigan had only been infatuation. She preferred to be by herself and was more relaxed and contented when he was not around. Still, as time passed she began to worry about him and looked increasingly for his return. She expected him to show up at any time. She realized, however, as the days grew shorter and colder with winter approaching, that she should prepare herself for the long cold days that lay ahead in case he didn't return when he said he would. She never saw him again.

She gathered in the potatoes by herself and cached them in a hole in the ground in the clearing to protect them from the frost. She chinked the gaps and cracks in the walls of the hovel with leaves and twigs and mud from the brook. She also stored away huge quantities of berries and wild fruit that she had picked on the hills and barrens just beyond the woods. She gathered fallen tree branches and chopped and piled them until she finally thought she had enough to last her a long time.

Christmas came and went, and there was still no sign of Ned Madigan. Hannah braced herself for a winter alone. Mercifully, her first winter in the hovel was milder than most, and she was somehow able to survive. Still, when spring finally came she was so gaunt, weak and lightheaded that she sometimes spent entire days just resting on the sleeping bench to conserve her waning strength and energy. The last of the potatoes and berries had run out, and she survived from day to day on the small speckled trout that she was able to catch from the brook, or by grubbing in the woods for roots and green plants. Reduced to such an extreme, she sometimes didn't know if what she ate was edible or not, or even cared.

That was three years ago. In that entire time frame, not a single person from the settlement had attempted to befriend her in any manner or had even spoken to her with anything other than scorn and contempt – except for the young priest who she thought had only recently arrived in the settlement himself, perhaps to replace the older priest she had seen earlier. He had dropped by to see her on five separate occasions, about once a month.

She sometimes thought it ironic that in this totally Roman Catholic enclave, only the spiritual head of the parish and the official representative of the Vatican itself saw fit to acknowledge her presence here among them.

On his second visit, after he had learned that she could read and write, the young priest had brought her some books to help her pass the time. He always brought her something, perhaps a loaf of bread, a fish or two, or some item of used clothing that he had collected from somewhere in his parish. On his last visit in late September, he had brought her a thick woolen blanket that she knew would keep her a little warmer in the winter months that would soon be upon her again. It was well worn and slightly raveled on one edge, but the priest had assured her that the person who had owned it no longer needed it.

He always told her what was happening in the parish and any news from abroad that he had heard. It was he who told her Ned Madigan had died in prison in St. John's. He couldn't tell her the nature of his crime, the length of his sentence, or the facts surrounding his death – he didn't know them himself. She was not overly shocked or unduly saddened by the news, and she told him all about herself and the circumstances of her arrival in Renews. He had also told her on his last visit about the rumors of the wild men out on the barrens, and advised her to be careful and vigilant, for if they were indeed out there and should decide to make a foray into Renews, hers would likely be the first house that they would pass on the way in.

At the end of each visit, before leaving, he would always say a short prayer with her. On one of his earlier visits, he had offered to instruct her for conversion to the Roman Catholic faith. Her Protestant upbringing was still too strong, however, and she had gracefully declined. He had understood and didn't press the matter any further. He also seemed grateful for the switchel tea that she gave him. He always drank it all, perhaps knowing that it was the best she had to offer.

After he had left the last time, she thought for a few minutes about what he had told her about the men in the wilderness. She recalled that on two or three occasions within the past few months, she had experienced the uncomfortable sensation that someone was watching her. She dismissed the idea quickly, however, knowing that it had surely been only her own overactive imagination.

sixteen

One night, shortly after Styles's brush with death, while Kerrivan and the other members of the outlaw band huddled in the warmth of their campfire trying to fend off the chill of the early December air, they were shaken when a voice hailed their camp and, before any of them could spring to their feet to douse the fire or prepare to defend themselves against whoever was coming, two young boys stepped into the firelight as nonchalantly as if they had come there by invitation. Finn was the first to react, and within the space of a few split seconds, before they had any chance to explain their presence there, the two jaunty newcomers found themselves wriggling helplessly in the iron grip of the big man's huge hands.

Kerrivan's first instinct was to wonder if the boys were alone or whether they had brought anybody else with them. How could they have found himself and the others here when, after all this time, nobody else, including the best tactical minds in the area, had been able to do so? It could certainly not be because he or any other member of the band had been negligent or lax in their vigilance, for John Shannahan, perhaps the most reliable of them all, was at that very moment taking his turn on watch. How could the boys possibly have slipped past him, even in the darkness? Unless he was asleep at his post, something that Kerrivan doubted, but which, if true, he would certainly do something about at the first opportunity.

Worried that this might be yet another ruse to catch him and the other members of the band off guard, he questioned the boys until he was fully satisfied that nobody else had come with them. When he listened to their story and understood the manner in which the boys had found their way into his camp, he threw back his head and laughed loudly and long.

He was amazed at the ingenuity and simplicity of the boys' plan. Despite his amusement and admiration, he was also sobered by the lesson that the two youngsters had taught him, and he resolved to take measures to ensure that it wouldn't happen again. For if two cocky young Irish lads had been able to find them so easily, it might not be long before someone else, someone posing a much greater threat to them than the boys, would do the same.

What the two boys told him, however, was not their full story. For the sequence of events that had led them here to the Butterpot mountain a few weeks before Christmas in 1750 had actually begun in Ireland many years earlier.

Patrick Duffy, who was never called anything but Paddy by anyone in his lifetime, either here or in Ireland, was the bigger and older of the two boys. At thirteen, he was slight of frame and his tousle of red hair made his puckish face seem smaller than it really was. When he was only eleven years of age, he had been awakened along with the rest of his family very early one morning when a gang of thugs descended upon them as they slept. They had been sent by the landowner who wanted the piece of ground on which Paddy and his family were squatting for some other more profitable purpose. The Duffys were forcibly evicted from their home and their few paltry possessions thrown out into the street. The terror that he had felt at the time, and the screams of his mother and his sisters and brothers, and his bewildered father standing mutely by trying to comprehend what was happening, were indelibly etched in his mind.

Several other families living nearby, all of whom were just as poverty stricken as Paddy's own, were dealt the same fate. He and his six brothers and sisters, along with his father and mother, had been forced to watch helplessly as the crude hut that they called home was "tumbled"[4] to the ground. With nowhere else to go, Paddy and his family had moved them-

---

[4] The practice of "tumbling," although perhaps prevalent at that time, would be employed on a wholesale scale across Ireland many years later, during the Great Potato Famine. It was the method used to evict millions of poor Irish men, women and children from their homes and drive them away to face a slow death of hunger and starvation, or in droves to America.

selves and their belongings into a ditch that they tried to cover as best they could with the remains of their razed cottage to keep out the rain. After only one day, however, they were driven from there too and told to leave the area immediately or face the even graver consequence of imprisonment.

Paddy and his family had then embarked on a transient existence across Ireland that saw them scavenging everywhere they went for food and shelter, as Paddy put it, "to try to keep ourselves on the right side of the sod." His father and older brothers searched in vain for work, except for an occasional odd job or 'hobble' that usually gave them employment for a day or two at the most.

Then, one after another within the space of a few short weeks, as their emaciated bodies grew steadily weaker from malnourishment and the ordeal of their travails across the country, his twin sisters, Mary and Eileen, only four, and his brother, James, aged seven, perished. Their deaths prompted Paddy to think that he might have a better chance of survival on his own. And perhaps his family's own odds for survival might be improved without having him to feed along with the three other remaining children. So one morning, while the rest of his family still slept, he left them and struck out alone.

Like Kerrivan, the man whom he had now come to join, he spent the next two and a half years of his life fending for himself in the green Irish countryside and in its grimy cities and towns, begging and stealing food and taking shelter wherever he could find it. Unlike Kerrivan, however, he never settled down in any one place, nor did he establish any lasting relationship with any of the thousands of other homeless children who were roaming Ireland at the same time. He preferred to go it alone – until he met a boy named O'Brien, another Patrick like himself, and, even more coincidently, another Paddy.

Paddy O'Brien, a year younger than Paddy Duffy, was from Antrim in the northern part of Ireland. His circumstances and background were not dissimilar to Duffy's own. The two boys hit it off from the start and became fast friends. After a few days, however, they agreed that having two Patrick's, let alone two Paddy's, was posing to be a bit of a problem, and that one of them should change his name to something else. When they drew straws to see who would be the one to do so, Paddy Duffy, who had initiated the idea in the first place, found himself holding the short piece.

Choosing a new name was not an easy or trivial matter, and Paddy Duffy took his time about it – two full days in fact. The names he came up with himself as well as those proposed by Paddy O'Brien were rejected one by one after much long and thoughtful deliberation. Perhaps, somewhere deep within his consciousness, Duffy saw the choosing of a new name as an opportunity to put behind him forever the hardship and misery of the first thirteen years of his young life, and perhaps more importantly, the chance for a fresh new start.

Finally, long after O'Brien had stopped offering suggestions because he had simply run out of names, as the two of them were munching on apples that they had just stolen from some farmer's tree, Duffy's eyes suddenly lit up and he proclaimed to his companion, "I got it, Paddy, I got it. Brian, that's what I'll be called from now on. Brian. Don't that sound grand to you, Paddy?"

He had chosen for his new name none other than that of Brian Boru, who had routed the fierce Norsemen from Ireland in the eleventh century and restored Ireland's religion and culture. Like most Irish boys, he had heard about the legendary warrior king at a very early age while sitting on his mother's lap.

With that important piece of business settled and out of the way, the two Paddy's, or more precisely, now Brian and Paddy, continued their meandering journey through Ireland, drifting ever southward toward Cork and Waterford where they hoped that life for them might be a little easier and the weather a little warmer. As they traveled toward their destination they began to hear stories about a great new country called America, a place where men treated each other as equals and where there was more than enough food for everybody. Everybody there, they were told, had work to do and a warm bed to go to each night. To the boys, it sounded like Paradise – and they made up their minds that America was where they would go.

Stowing away on a ship leaving Ireland for England proved to be a relatively simple matter, and within the space of a few weeks of making their decision to leave Ireland, they found themselves in the bustling English port of Bristol. But it would be almost another three months before they were finally able to stow away on a ship bound for America, by which time they were both much thinner and gaunter than they had been when they first arrived in the seaport city. They found the pickings of Bristol much slimmer than they had in Ireland where, if nothing else, they could always manage to lay their hands on a few potatoes.

On their second day at sea, while they were both being violently seasick, they had been discovered in their hiding place in one of the ship's lifeboats and brought to the captain. Fortunately for them, the captain was a kindly man who knew firsthand what motivated boys to become stowaways, for he had been a stowaway himself at one time. He simply put the boys to work on the ship, fed them, and when they arrived in Ferryland three weeks later, led them smartly to the garrison and turned them over to Lieutenant Stanford.

Brian Duffy and Paddy O'Brien were in the garrison in the Ferryland Plantation for almost a week before they discovered that they were not in America, but in Newfoundland. Still, life in the garrison, where they now had more food and comfort than they had ever known, was infinitely better than their life had been in Ireland. They even had cots to sleep in at night with the men in the barracks. They were contented to bide their time there and postpone trying to get to America for another time.

Having arrived shortly before the Shannahans made their escape, Brian and Paddy heard the same stories as the brothers had about Kerrivan and his outlaw band. And they were enthralled. They themselves were not prisoners like the Shannahans had been, or confined to the same extent as the indentured servants of the plantation. They had some semblance of freedom and were both free to come and go as they pleased as long as they did the chores that were assigned to them and behaved themselves. Nor, for the first time in their lives, were they hungry. Still, as they continued to listen to the stories, the lure of the outlaw band proved too irresistible and they too, like John and Liam Shannahan, decided to leave the security and comfort of the garrison and try to find their way to the outlaws' hideout.

Unlike the Shannahans, they did not need to wait for a suitable opportunity to flee. When they had made up their minds, they simply walked out through the garrison gate, exchanged pleasantries with the guard on duty, and kept going. Like the numerous contingents of men who had made earlier attempts to find and rout the outlaws from their lair, Brian and Paddy made their way across the barrens toward the Butterpot mountain under the cover of darkness so that their approach would not be detected, and dawn found them hiding in a clump of trees near the base of the mountain. Instead of then proceeding to search for the outlaw band in the morning, as the others before them had done, the boys remained in their hiding place all that day until it was dark again.

When they then finally proceeded to the mountain itself in the moonlight, they climbed its eastern side until they were well over half way to the top. There they waited again, hoping that from their viewpoint overlooking the area below they might see some sign of the outlaws if they were, as everyone was saying, living anywhere near the mountain. Surely they reasoned, if the men were on guard for trespassers, their attention would be focused on the barrens to the east, not behind them, and certainly not up on the mountain itself.

After only a couple of hours of waiting, the simple strategy of the boys paid off. When the first faint whiff of smoke, barely discernable, touched their nostrils, the boys left their perch and followed their noses until they were close enough to hear the voices of the outlaws in their camp, and see the warm orange glow of their campfire.

Then, knowing nothing better to do, they had simply walked in – and life within the outlaw band would never again be the same.

seventeen

P hilip Percival Stanford's cultured fingers stroked the polished surface of the large umber-stained oak table upon which rested the silver service that was reserved for the purpose of wining and dining visiting dignitaries and senior naval officers, like Captain Joshua Smith, whose ships put into Ferryland several times each year. The fourteen leather-backed chairs that encircled the table were meticulously arranged in perfect symmetry, as were the dozen oil paintings that adorned the paneled walls of the largest room of the garrison. Mostly seascapes and pastoral scenes depicting the typical English countryside, the paintings had all been done by prominent English artists, and were of some considerable value. The rich leather davenport, upon which he sometimes took an afternoon nap, the intricately carved cherry cabinet which housed curios of all kinds, and the large glass-fronted bookcase that contained more than a hundred leather-bound volumes, were the only ones of their kind in the settlement. Even the two Roman Catholic priests, who lived like czars in the large Presbytery on the top of the hill at the expense of the settlers, had nothing to match them.

This room, with its treasures, was Lieutenant Stanford's sanctuary, his private domain, the only thing that enabled him to maintain his sanity among the foul-smelling and even fouler-mouthed settlers, predominantly Irish Roman Catholics, who populated the God-forsaken plantation in which he had spent the last long eleven years of his life.

His disdain for the settlers extended in almost equal measure to his own officers and men, most of whom he viewed as being as coarse and as ignorant as the settlers themselves. Here, alone except for the company of the decanter of Irish whiskey that always rested along with a few crystal tumblers on the sideboard (at least the Irish were good for something) was where he spent most of his free time. Very infrequently, except on formal occasions, did any of his officers, or anyone else for that matter, join him here. Even his wife, Martha, whom he had stopped loving many years ago, if indeed he had ever done so, seldom entered the room.

Philip Stanford was a loner. He hadn't always been one. When he had first been posted to the Ferryland Plantation in Newfoundland eleven years earlier, where many men before him had proven their worth and gone on to greater things, he had been a motivated and energetic officer, who saw his assignment to the plantation as a short-stayed stepping stone to higher promotion and other more exotic postings. But when the anticipated promotions had not materialized within his expected time-frame, he had become increasingly disillusioned and gradually developed into the embittered recluse who now rarely enjoyed any company other than his own. And he continued to languish in Ferryland year after year despite his repeated efforts to get himself recalled to England and reassigned somewhere else, hopefully somewhere more civilized and cultured than this inhospitable speck on the Southern Shore of Newfoundland. He couldn't understand why, after all this time, they hadn't sent a proper naval governor to replace him.

He hadn't slept in his wife's bed in almost seven years, and the rearing and education of his two daughters, Mina and Victoria, aged eleven and nine respectively, were almost totally left to Martha. He sometimes thought that the two girls were becoming more like their mother with every passing day, and they, perceiving his remoteness as a lack of fatherly affection for them, usually kept their distance. Still, there were moments when he regretted having not developed a better relationship with them, especially head-strong and adventurous Victoria, in whom he saw a bit of himself in his earlier years. Mina, on the other hand, was demure and very womanly in her ways. Although he hadn't gone out of his way to tell them, he would have been glad of their company on many of the long, cold evenings that he had spent here.

When Captain Smith had sailed away in the *Fortress* the previous spring without having recaptured the three men who had escaped from his custody while the large frigate lay at anchor in Ferryland Harbour, Stanford had himself made a couple of halfhearted attempts to track down the men whom everyone along the coast believed were still at large out in the wilderness. Unlike Smith, however, who felt that the three escaped prisoners were the very scum of the earth and deserved nothing less than hanging, Stanford bore the missing men no personal malice. He had never met them or even laid eyes on them, and even though he was the highest-ranking representative of British law in the region in the absence of a resident Naval Governor, he did not as yet view the matter of the escaped prisoners as his problem. His token forays into the wilderness to search them out had been undertaken as much for appearances as they had been intended to actually try to find and capture the men.

The escape of the Shannahan brothers from right under his nose was an entirely different matter. He, like Smith, had been furious with the officers and men who had permitted it to happen. Not only was the escape of the men an embarrassment to him, the unexpected loss of two of his more capable workers was a severe blow to the daily functioning of the garrison itself.

However, as time passed and the bitter taste of the escape began to leave his mouth, Stanford gradually came around to the view that the departure of the brothers may have, in fact, been a blessing in disguise. He started to see the matter of the renegades in the wilderness in an entirely different light. For it had slowly dawn on him that perhaps the outlaw band was his ticket out of this place. If he could bring them to heel and in doing so serve British justice well, something which even the capable Captain Smith had been unable to do, he might finally bring upon himself the recognition that would remind his superiors back in England that he was still out here and deserving of some more important posting elsewhere. Consequently, he applied himself to the task of finding the missing men.

He knew that it would be nothing but an exercise in futility to continue to simply send out contingent after contingent of soldiers from the garrison to search for the outlaws, for they had undoubtedly buried themselves so deeply in some lair in the wilderness by this time that it would be virtually impossible to find them no matter how often and how long he might search. In any event, he did not have the manpower to commit a large number of his officers and men to the effort. They were all needed in the daily functioning of the garrison and the governing and maintenance of the plantation itself. Instead, he sent two of his officers to the nearby settlements of Fermeuse, Aquaforte, Renews, and Cappahayden to hear firsthand the stories and rumors about the men that had been circulating along this section of the coast for some months now. He was certain that somewhere in the information that his officers would bring back would be the clue that he needed to accomplish his goal.

And equally important, while his officers were thus engaged in their assignment, he himself wrote a long dispatch to his commanding officers in England in which he presented a grossly exaggerated account of the outlaw band and the havoc that it was wreaking upon the area.

In committing himself to rid the settlements under his jurisdiction of the terrible scourge that was terrorizing the population, Stanford knew full well that he was running the risk that if he failed to deliver what he promised, he would be buried here forever. He was also careful in his dispatches to employ the judicious use of phrases such as, "in my many years here," and, "since I first came here in 1739," or, "in my next posting," to remind his superiors that he, Lieutenant Philip Stanford, had served more than his allotted time here, and was long overdue for recall and reappointment to another command somewhere else – anywhere else.

He also had one of his officers post notices throughout the Ferryland Plantation and the other nearby settlements offering a reward of ten shillings, a king's ransom to the poor settlers of the area, for any information that would ultimately lead to the capture of the members of the outlaw band. The same notice informed anyone who read it that any man or woman found to be aiding and abetting the criminals in any manner would themselves be arrested and punished to the full extent of the law. It also made it perfectly clear that the outlaws, when taken, would be hanged in public with all due ceremony, regardless of the nature of their original crimes or the length of their earlier sentences, or any other circumstances notwithstanding. Not one of them would be spared.

The officers that Stanford had sent out into the settlements did their work well. They talked to every man, woman and child who thought they might have something of relevance to offer. They recorded everything, even though much of it was so obviously improbable and farfetched as to be immediately discarded out of hand. They would let Stanford himself be the judge of what was credible and what was not.

According to the information that they gathered, the outlaws had been seen everywhere, sometimes in two or more places at the same time. The things that the men had stolen ranged from items of food and clothing to animals, hens and sheep, a musket, even jugs of fermenting wine. The savage acts that they had supposedly performed during their pillaging forays into the settlements extended from the vandalizing of houses, fences, outbuildings, and boats to bodily assault and murder, although not a single injured or dead body could be produced anywhere in the area to support this claim. Not one of the settlements from the Ferryland Plantation to Cappahayden seemed to have been spared a visit or two by the marauding outlaw band.

As the officers sifted through the details that had been provided to them, three points had enough of a common thread to make them stand out from everything else. Firstly, the outlaws, while they had supposedly raided at some time or other every settlement in the area, appeared to have singled out Renews as their favorite and most frequent target. Secondly, almost every settler to whom they had talked was convinced that the men were living on the Butterpot mountain. Some even claimed that they had seen the smoke of the outlaws' campfire out there in the distance. And thirdly, the repeated reference to two men in particular, one of them tall, blond and blue-eyed and the other a huge bearded hulk of a man, prompted the officers to think that there was perhaps some truth in what they were being told after all.

In any event, they spent the better part of two weeks interviewing settlers before wrapping up their investigative sojourn through the settlements. At one point, before returning to the garrison and presenting their findings to Lieutenant Stanford, they themselves even walked out to the beginning of the wilderness area and spent some time surveying the mountain in the distance. They had not, however, as they had perhaps hoped, seen smoke, movement, or any other sign of life anywhere on the vast sweep of barren ground that stretched out before them.

Hour after hour, Stanford pored over the information that his officers brought back to him. He arranged the pages of their report on the large dining table so that he could find anything that he was looking for without having to leaf through the pages each time. He had read and reread the summary that the two men had prepared so many times that he knew its content by heart. Even though he didn't tell the officers, he had to grudgingly admit to himself that they had done a commendable piece of work. Still, he continued to sift through the rough notes that they had taken to record the settlers' comments. He hoped to find something, some small shred somewhere that, irrelevant as it might seem, might nevertheless be important, something that his officers had perhaps missed or overlooked. He spent almost as much time trying to decipher the officers' poor handwriting and interpreting their misspelled words and disjointed sentences as he did on digesting the information itself that the report contained. He could not, however, find anything that his officers had not already covered in their summary.

The only other item in the notes that caught his attention was the statement by of one of the settlers of Renews that the outlaw band had by now at least a dozen members, if not more, and that they possessed an arsenal of weapons large enough to withstand any assault against them – or to carry out an attack of their own if they chose to do so.

Stanford briefly considered this piece of information before dismissing it as being highly improbable, if not impossible. Assuming that the Shannahan brothers had joined the outlaws, as everybody, including himself, thought was the case, that would mean that there were now at least five of them out there. Even in the unlikely event that another man, or even two, more improbable still, had somehow managed to join the band, that would still give them only six or seven men at the most. Hardly the small army that the settler had indicated. And where, indeed, could they have gotten such weapons? Nowhere in the area, that was for certain. The only significant supply of arms and ammunition along this entire stretch of coastline was that of the garrison itself.

As an officer he understood the importance of knowing the strength of the enemy, and he would take no foolish risk or precipitate action without having first satisfied himself that he had every possible bit of information at his disposal. Particularly in this case, because with only twelve or fourteen men of his own at the most to deploy in his campaign against the outlaw band, he could not mount a very large assault against them without depleting the garrison totally and letting the prisoners and indentured servants have free rein while his men were away.

He even considered the two Irish boys who had left the garrison shortly after the departure of the Shannahan brothers, but quickly dismissed the notion that the boys too might have joined the outlaw band. Even if they had done so, it caused him no great concern for they were only boys, mere children. Undoubtedly they had long since made their way to St. John's or had perhaps stowed away on some ship bound for America. During their stay in the garrison, he had never viewed them as prisoners or seen any reason to keep them confined. They had simply been two youths who had been placed in his custody by a visiting naval captain who had discovered them as stowaways on his ship. Even though the boys helped out with chores around the garrison and sometimes ran errands for Stanford and his officers, they were really nothing more to him than two extra mouths to feed, and when they left the garrison, Stanford had been glad enough to be rid of them.

When he decided that he had studied the findings of his officers long enough and knew as much as there was to know, he began to lay his plans. Although he had not been able to come up with anything new, he concluded that the information that he did have was perhaps all that he really needed. For he had some idea, at least, of where the outlaws might be holed up, and a reasonable estimate of their numbers. He even knew their names and their descriptions. He knew the Shannahan brothers firsthand and Captain Smith, before leaving, had given him a good description of the other three men. That was more than some of history's greatest generals had before they led their armies into battle with the enemy. And Stanford, with his military background and training, now viewed the men in the wilderness as just that – the enemy.

Still, he was cautious. Another commanding officer might have opted for an immediate all-out offensive against the mountain itself. But Stanford deemed that to be an option that he would reserve as a last resort. In his own estimation, intelligence and smart thinking had won more battles than hasty brute force, and he would first try to out-think the outlaws and bring the matter to an end without risking too many of his limited manpower resources. The garrison was already severely under-manned and he needed every last man for other things. Therefore, before deploying the full contingent of men that he had selected for his venture, he once again sent out his two officers to do some more advanced scouting. This time out into the wilderness itself, accompanied by two settlers whom everyone in the plantation said were the plantation's best hunters and most able trackers.

Stanford's objective was to have them scour the barrens for any signs that might indicate where the outlaws may have passed or spent some time. Even though the missing men had made their escape across the barrens several months earlier, perhaps the path they had followed might still somehow be evident and shed some light on the outlaws' whereabouts. The officers and the settlers were told not to return to the garrison until they had combed the entire area between the coast and the mountain, an area of some twenty-five square miles or more.

At the end of two full days in the wilderness area, the four men had nothing to show for their efforts. They started out at first light each morning, and continued their search until nightfall, crisscrossing each section of barrens several times to make sure that they had missed nothing. They returned each night to the camp that they had set up at the edge of the woods so that they would be ready to go out again as early as possible the next morning if need be.

Then, on the third day their painstaking diligence was finally rewarded when one of the settlers came upon the blackened remains of what had clearly been a recent campfire. A few animal bones and broken twigs and alders indicated that someone had stopped and eaten a meal there, and perhaps even slept there. A hundred yards further along they found two distinct footprints in a small patch of boggy ground, one of them very large, the other much smaller, indicating that at least two men had passed this way not long ago. Even more significant was the fact that the footprints were pointed in the direction of the mountain.

Further along they found a few more footprints. The officers were hopeful that they had finally picked up the trail of the outlaws. The trackers were not so sure. The trail that they were following could just as easily be that of some hunters or woodsmen from one of the nearby settlements, although both men knew that settlers from the coast seldom ventured this far out in search of game or timber. Instead, they usually concentrated their efforts on the closer forested area that ran parallel to the coast, where they stood a much greater chance of finding what they were looking for.

After another half hour of searching, they found the spot where some human had emptied his bowels, a few more footprints, and a small piece of cloth caught in the sharp branches of an alder. The two trackers were themselves beginning to think by now that the trail they were following might indeed be that of the outlaws. They intensified their efforts, taking every precaution to make sure that they didn't lose it. And finally, to their amazement, they came upon several sets of footprints in another damp area that told them that at least three men had traveled over the wet ground in which they were set. The footprints stretched out in an unbroken line toward the mountain. They were so plainly evident that the men who had trod there had made no attempt whatsoever to conceal them. It was virtually impossible to lose them now, and the anticipation of the four men was greatly heightened.

Five minutes later, however, they were puzzled, and then

stunned, when the footprints that they were following led straight into a pond about a mile and a half distant from the mountain. They could find no evidence anywhere that they had ever again emerged from the small body of water. Their frantic search around the full circumference of the pond and the surrounding area proved fruitless. The trail had run out, and the officers and the two settlers realized that they had been duped. They had followed a trail deliberately set for them, designed to frustrate them and lead them somewhere other than to the true location of the outlaws' hideout.

Chagrined and disheartened after all their work, they returned to their camp and made plans for the following day. And later that day, they found more footprints. They suspected, even as they followed them, that it was yet another blind trail set by the outlaws to deliberately mislead and confuse them. After more than two hours of halfhearted walking, their suspicions were confirmed when the trail again petered out, this time into a small copse of twisted juniper and spruce trees.

When the officers and the trackers returned to their base camp for the last time, they conceded that the outlaws they were searching for were intelligent men, undoubtedly more cunning than themselves, and that the task of finding them and dislodging them from their place of concealment would not be an easy one. Explaining this to Lieutenant Stanford, however, would be another matter. Still, there was nothing else to do, but to return to the garrison and face his wrath for having failed in their objective.

Curiously, Stanford was not as angry as they had expected him to be. They were both greatly relieved when he dismissed them with what they considered to be little more than a token dressing down. They had been braced for much worse. Neither of them realized that Stanford, despite his hopes to the contrary, had not harbored any real expectations that they would bring back any concrete evidence of the outlaws' whereabouts. The stories that the people of the settlements had recounted about the boldness and audacity of the outlaws' raids had already told him that these were no ordinary escaped prisoners that he was dealing with. And the descriptions of the two men that the settlers had spoken about most often told him that they were undoubtedly Kerrivan and Finn.

In any case, the search of the barrens carried out by his officers had not been a complete waste of time. If nothing else, the existence of the false trails verified the fact that the outlaws must indeed still be out there somewhere. The trails also told him that they were digging in for the long haul, and taking every precaution to protect themselves against all comers and to prevent themselves from being found and recaptured.

Realizing that he now had no recourse but to mount the assault on the mountain that he had been postponing, he gathered his officers together in the dining room, which by this time was used for no purpose other than Stanford's battle headquarters, and laid out his plans.

Two days later he sent his full contingent of men to the mountain. Like Captain Smith, he had ordered them to cross the barrens under the cover of darkness so that they would be at or near the mountain when the day broke. After ten hours of searching, however, they were unable to find any trace of the missing men. By early afternoon, they couldn't even tell whether the signs that they did come across had been made by the outlaws or by themselves after their hours of fruitless tramping around the base of the mountain and upon its slopes. They too returned to the garrison as empty-handed as their officers had in their own earlier failed attempt to find Kerrivan and the others.

Stanford, after he had listened to their account of the fruitless foray and lambasted them for their failure, sent them away. And retired, without undressing, to spend the night on the davenport, fuming and sleepless, until the whiskey from the decanter at his elbow finally took him into its soothing embrace.

eighteen

May, 1751, marked the end of the outlaw band's first year in the wilderness of the Southern Shore. Having barely survived their first winter on the Butterpot mountain, they were much thinner and weaker than they had been before the onset of the cold winter months, and spent much of their time in the indentation in the cliff just trying to keep themselves warm. The snow and frost that had begun in early January stayed until the end of February, effectively curtailing their raids into the settlements for almost two full months. Despite the fact that they had come to rely on their forays into Renews, Fermeuse and the other nearby settlements for their survival, Kerrivan and the other members of the band knew that they could not run the risk of leaving a trail in the snow that could easily be followed back to their hideout. An unseasonably warm spell in the last few days of February took away the snow for a period of two weeks, and Kerrivan and the other members of the band, except the two Irish boys, Brian and Paddy, took advantage of this temporary respite to make their first raid in months. Kerrivan was reluctant to take the boys with him because of their inexperience and youthful exuberance, and left them behind with Styles to keep watch on the mountain.

Unfortunately, the raid into Renews, chosen because it was there that they had met with the most success in the past, netted them nothing this time to improve their precarious lot in the wilderness in any meaningful way. Other than the armful of heavily-salted, half-frozen codfish that they took from one of the fishing rooms on the beach, they returned to the mountain empty-handed. And, before they could make another foray into one of the other settlements, the weather grew cold again and newly fallen snow once more covered the barrens, isolating Kerrivan and the others for another five weeks in their lair at the base of the Butterpot mountain.

The long period of near starvation, inactivity, and numbing cold took its toll on the band. Even John Shannahan's stories and the childish antics of Brian Duffy and Paddy O'Brien could not dispel the cloud of gloom and depression that descended on them while they waited for the long days of winter to pass. They had never imagined that winter could be this bad. Within the close confines of the indentation, the men, cold, hungry, dirty, and lice-ridden, grew increasing argumentative and testy with each other, and it sometimes taxed Kerrivan's leadership and patience to the limit to keep them from going at each other with fists or knives. Styles, the most likely target of the others even when he had done nothing in particular to provoke them, was careful to keep himself in the background as much as possible and to stay uninvolved in whatever was happening around him.

It had also been Father Fabian O'Donnell's first winter in Newfoundland. Unlike Kerrivan, Finn, Styles, and the other members of the outlaw band, however, he had spent the cold winter months in the warmth and comfort of the Presbytery. Despite his more comfortable surroundings and the fact that he had food on his table every day, the winter had nevertheless been a lonely one for the young priest.

His work in the parish kept him busy during the days. It was the nights that he had to spend all alone in the Presbytery that were the problem. All his life he had always been surrounded by people, by his family in Claras Graen and by his fellow students and the priests and bishops of the Waterford seminary. The long winter nights in the Presbytery, during which he seldom had any visitors or callers except to be informed when someone in the parish had passed away or to be told that he was needed to visit some sick or dying parishioner, had been an unfulfilling experience, and as the winter lengthened he had found himself increasingly yearning for the company of other human beings.

Sometimes, on clear nights when the moon and stars shone brightly enough to enable him to find his way around easily, he took long walks around the settlement, hoping perhaps that someone among the people he passed along the way would see fit to invite him in for a cup of tea or a chat. Only rarely, however, did that happen and on most nights he returned to the empty Presbytery after walking around by himself for an hour or more. He knew that he could have called upon any of the families in the four settlements that comprised his parish at any time and would have been welcomed in, but he did not wish to intrude or impose himself on anyone. He had earlier sensed that many of his parishioners, while they always greeted him warmly and appeared to like and respect him, were not entirely comfortable in his presence for any extended period of time. He remembered hearing two of the priests back in the Seminary discussing the same thing about their relationship with the poor Irish families of Waterford County.

So, apart from an occasional outing when he simply could not stand another moment alone in the Presbytery, he contented himself with reading the books that Father Connolly had left, except those that he had loaned to Hannah Martin and had not yet gotten back, and by writing letters and dispatches to his family and his superiors in Waterford, knowing as he did so that it would be quite some time yet before the first ships of spring would be able to carry them back to England and Ireland for him.

The supply of firewood that he had laid in the previous fall had been more than sufficient for his winter needs. After the first few nights, during which he had felt too warm and uncomfortable in bed, he stopped using the fireplace in the upstairs bedroom. He preferred instead to pile on all the blankets that he found in the Presbytery to keep his body warm in the cold, sometimes freezing room, while he enjoyed the feel of the frigid night air on his exposed head and face. On some nights he left his window slightly open and often awoke to the strangely pleasant feeling of tiny flecks of snow or ice on his skin.

On the coldest nights, as many of the settlers in the area were in the habit of doing, he heated stones downstairs in the kitchen fireplace and carried them, wrapped in cloth, upstairs and placed them under the coverings of his bed so that the bed would be warm and cozy when he retired for the night.

The monotony of the long cold winter had been broken on a couple of occasions. Firstly, during the twelve days of Christmas which the settlers of the parish celebrated with great enthusiasm. Their yuletide activities included the practice of mummering, a custom brought over from the old country by their forebears many years earlier. In the spirit of the Christmas season, Father Fabian had been invited to many of the homes in the parish and treated to the special food and liquor that the settlers had been hoarding for the yuletide period. He had only been able to laugh when one man in the group of mummers who had showed up at the Presbytery door on Boxing Day, already more than a little intoxicated from his earlier visits to other houses in the settlement, and had been offered a cup of steaming tea by the young priest, told him, "Ah now Father, me dear, you're a nice little man but you'll have to do a lot better than that. Sure I can get a bloody cup of tea in me own house anytime I wants one."

Unable to offer the man and his companions anything stronger, Father Fabian had made a mental note to himself to acquire some spirits for other such future occasions.

Then in mid-March, he had been invited to the St. Patrick's Day soiree down in Cappahayden. There he turned a deaf ear to the raucous songs and the ribald stories of the men and women and a blind eye to much of what was going on around him, and enjoyed himself to the limit for a few hours.

For Hannah Martin, the winter of 1751, her fourth in the hovel in the clearing since arriving there from Harbour Grace, was the easiest one yet. Her stores of potatoes, berries, and other preserves held out and she emerged from the winter, although thin and somewhat weary, in much better condition, both physically and mentally, than in previous years. The thick woolen blanket that Father Fabian had given her in the fall had kept her much warmer during the cold weather, and the books that he had loaned her had sustained her as much as her supply of food through the long lonely days and nights. She read them all, some of them several times, losing herself in their contents and forgetting everything else for hours at a time. Still, she thought that some of the books, particularly Chaucers's Canterbury Tales and Robin Hood of Sherwood Forest, were odd literary choices for a Roman Catholic Priest.

The young priest had visited her twice during the winter months, slogging the two miles from his own door to the clearing in the woods through the slush and snow to bring her a few morsels of food and another book or two each time. His was the only company that she knew for the entire winter period, except for the odd settler that passed by her door on his way to hunt or to cut wood. She had particularly enjoyed their discussion about some of the books that she had read before returning them to him.

The arrival of fine spring weather in late April and early May was a blessing to them all – the outlaws in the wilderness, Father Fabian, Hannah Martin, and indeed all of the other men, women and children of the Southern Shore for whom winter was always the hardest time of the year.

When the barrens around the base of the Butterpot mountain came alive with the colors of spring, budding new growth, and teeming wildlife, so too did Brian Duffy and Paddy O'Brien. The natural high spirits of the boys had been held in check for most of the winter by the effort of keeping themselves warm and alive like the other members of the outlaw band. Now, with the release of their pent-up exuberance and vivacity, they took to their new home in the wilderness like ducks to a millpond. Their energy and vitality knew no limits. Always wild and seldom disciplined in their childhood years, they were now wilder and freer still. They chased each other and wrestled with each other from dawn to dusk, pausing only to flop in the goowithy and gorse when they could go no longer. With absolute freedom, enough food to eat now that the winter was over, and the protection, perhaps even affection, of the men in the band, they were children in the Garden of Eden. They had never known such happiness and contentment in their lives.

And when they tired of each other, they turned their attention to the men and teased and tormented them mercilessly without let up. Nobody except Styles escaped their shenanigans. They made Finn, the biggest and fiercest of them all, their favorite target. The big man's threats to wring their necks and his never quite successful attempts to collar them had little effect other than to spur them on and incite them to even further extremes. They didn't bother Styles because they knew instinctively that he would not abide their pranks like the other men who, despite themselves, invariably ended up laughing even when they themselves had been made the butt of one of the boys' practical jokes or pranks.

Besides bringing an element of zest and brightness to the long days of the men in the wilderness, the boys also brought a measure of usefulness to the band. In their short stay, they had already become much more adept and skilled at catching trout from the pond and in snaring rabbits, birds and other small animals than the men, and assumed that daily duty themselves, keeping the larder in the wilderness well-stocked at all times. Both of them also had fine clear voices and loved to sing. The area around the base of the mountain reverberated from morning to night with the sounds of their songs and ditties and the rollicking Irish tunes that the Shannahan brothers taught them.

The rest of that year was a repetition of the outlaws' first summer and fall in the wilderness. Their continued raids into the settlements made life for the settlers who lived there miserable, and despite their best efforts to protect their few possessions, many of the things that they owned and treasured most still wound up on the Butterpot mountain. The band successfully eluded Lieutenant Stanford's repeated attempts to find and capture them, and Kerrivan and the other members of the outlaw band continued to grow bolder and more daring in their endeavors.

Kerrivan's own strange fascination with Hannah Martin prompted him to stop for a few minutes whenever he passed through the woods, hoping to catch a glimpse of her at her work in the clearing. He felt a keen sense of disappointment on the few occasions when he hadn't seen her at all. The last time he had paused at the edge of the clearing he had been certain that she had spotted him as he made no attempt to hide or leave when she looked his way. He didn't realize that she had already seen him on a prior occasion when he had stopped there for a few minutes several weeks earlier.

Hannah, at the time, had not felt afraid or threatened in any way by his presence, and realized that her earlier sensations of being watched had not been unfounded after all. She had even been tempted to approach him and speak to him, but before she could do so he was gone.

For the outlaws, Father Fabian, and Hannah Martin, 1751

was a year of relative peace and tranquility. It wasn't until the following year that a sequence of events would come into play that would grip the settlements of Ferryland, Aquaforte, Fermeuse, Cappahayden, and especially Renews, in a siege of terror and divide the outlaw band.

nineteen

By early 1752, word of the existence of the outlaw band in the wilderness of the Southern Shore had spread to other parts of Newfoundland, including the bustling port of St. John's fifty miles to the north of the Ferryland Plantation. The month of May, the second anniversary of Kerrivan's, Finn's, and Styles' own arrival on the Southern Shore, brought with it, in the person of Nate Johnson, another newcomer to the band. He was the first of a trickle of men that would make their way to the Butterpot mountain that year to swell the size of the band to eleven, one shy of fulfilling the estimate offered to Lieutenant Stanford's officers by the settler in Renews a year earlier, all wanting to join Kerrivan's band of lawless men, each with his own reason for doing so.

Johnson, a bantam Cockney from the east end of London, whose cruel and violent nature belied his diminutive appearance, had bolted from St. John's after carving up an unarmed man in a vicious brawl on the waterfront in full view of dozens of witnesses. He had then made his way to the Ferryland Plantation, and subsequently to the mountain in the wilderness, by various means, over a period of seven or eight days.

His victim in St. John's had not been the first to feel the point of Johnson's knife. Johnson had left a trail of violent crime behind him wherever he had gone since his first armed robbery and assault in London fifteen years earlier. With the law breathing down his neck and facing the prospect of imprisonment and possibly hanging in England, he fled to Newfoundland in 1749 and, by his cunning and the force of his predatory nature, survived the ensuing three-year period in the streets and back alleys of St. John's with a number of companions of his own ilk.

Although Kerrivan, Finn, and the Shannahan brothers, even the two Irish boys, had almost immediately recognized him as a misfit in the band, Johnson had on his very first day on the mountain formed a close relationship with Styles, in whom he had instantly detected a kindred spirit. After only a few days in the hideout location, he and Styles moved their bedding and their few personal effects to another part of the indentation in the cliff, effectively isolating themselves from the other members of the band.

Still, Johnson did bring something to the band besides his violent and sadistic nature, something that Kerrivan and the others did not have before – a musical instrument, a lute on which, in his less surly moments, he could play amazingly beautiful tunes. On many nights, as the original members of the band sat around the fire making plans or discussing the events of the day, or simply swapping stories, the sweet refrain of Green Sleeves or some other soulful classic, always soft and moving, would invariably waft from the far corner of the indentation in the cliff where Johnson and Styles now kept their own company, filling the cool night air of the mountain with its bittersweet melancholy.

Johnson's lute playing, when he was in the mood, made a beautiful complement to the crystal clear voices of the boys, and there were moments at the base of the Butterpot mountain that brought tears to the eyes of the men, especially the softhearted Shannahan brothers. There were also moments when Johnson shed his nasty temperament and interacted with the other members of the band in a pleasant, friendly, almost cordial manner. The others, puzzled by his psychotic behavior, themselves vacillated between dislike and an occasional moment of acceptance for the new man, never quite sure how to take him.

The first indication of the element of wanton disregard for life and property that Johnson would introduce into the band's forays into the settlements became evident on his second raid with the other members of the band. Having scoured the darkened community of Aquaforte and fulfilled the purpose of their nocturnal visit, Kerrivan, Finn, and the others had started to make their way back to the mountain when Johnson suddenly left them and went back into the sleeping settlement, telling them that he would catch up with them in a few minutes. When he eventually caught up with them a short while later, they were puzzled by the dramatic change in his appearance. Glassy-eyed, red-faced, blood-splattered, breathing heavily and sweating profusely, he seemed strangely exhilarated and aroused.

In answer to their questions, he told Kerrivan and the other men only that he had wanted to check on something. He did not bother to tell them that he had just methodically slaughtered the dozen or so roosting hens that he had spied in one of the chicken coops that the band passed on its way out of the settlement, leaving their bloody and twisted bodies strewn around the small enclosure in the manner of a marauding fox or weasel or some other predatory creature. He hadn't even thought to bring one or two of the destroyed birds back with him for them to eat. His only motivation had been the sheer joy of killing and inflicting pain. With his bloodlust sated for the moment, he whistled softly to himself all the way back to the mountain.

A month after Johnson's arrival, two other newcomers made their way into the outlaw band. Both deserters from the British Navy, like Kerrivan himself, they had jumped ship in St. John's weeks earlier. Gabriel Foley, a brawling Irishman from Kilkenny, and the introverted William Shaheen, also Irish, had, after a year of service on the *Crusader*, made a conscious decision that they would no longer tolerate the abuse and maltreatment of the predominantly British crew, and made their unsuspected departure while on shore leave in the capital port.

Both Foley and Shaheen immediately sensed the rift in the band and threw in their lot with Johnson and Styles, widening the chasm between the two factions ever further. Johnson, by himself, was capable of unspeakably cruel and violent acts. The combination of the four men, however, with their collective appetite for viciousness and brutality, was a recipe for mayhem and destruction on a scale never before witnessed on the Southern Shore. The raids of the band from that point onward took on a new dimension, escalating beyond mere thievery to widespread property damage, bodily harm to a number of settlers in Ferryland and the other four settlements comprising the Renews Parish, and, eventually, murder.

twenty

The fateful year of 1752 was also one of great significance for Hannah Martin. For the first time since arriving from Harbour Grace, she became ill. Despite the harsh conditions under which she had lived for the previous four years in the clearing in the woods and the biting cold winds that sometimes numbed her to the bone, she had never been seriously ill before. The periods of bone-weary fatigue and lightheadedness that she experienced each spring had always been induced by her near state of starvation at that time of the year, and had always disappeared with the onset of warmer weather and an improved diet. This time it was very different.

It was while she was kneeling among her potatoes, pulling weeds and pushing a handful of fresh soil against the semi-exposed roots of an occasional plant as she inspected her new crop, that she was suddenly stopped short by an unbearably intense pain in her neck and chest area that, with great clarity and detached objectivity, she immediately assumed to be a heart attack. Within the matter of only a minute or two, despite the relative warmth of the pleasant September morning, her body was covered with cold sweat and a bone-numbing chill sent uncontrollable paroxysms through her body, incapacitating her where she knelt. The ground swam before her eyes and her limbs felt strangely separate from the rest of her body. She tried to rise to her feet, to attempt to make her way back to the hut so that she could lie down and rest. Her initial effort failed, and before she could try again, she felt suffocating blackness washing over her, and despite her efforts to fight it, fell into the vegetables that she had been tending only minutes earlier, unconscious even before her face hit the soft ground.

She was a victim of a small isolated outbreak of an unknown disease with bubonic plague-like symptoms that swept over this short stretch of the Southern Shore to claim the lives of a number of men, women and children in the area. On a scale minuscule in comparison to the great epidemic that had killed thousands in London in the previous century and had only been finally eradicated by the virtual burning of the great city, the disease had probably been brought to Renews by a rat on a visiting ship and then transmitted throughout the surrounding settlements by the blackflies and mosquitoes that constantly buzzed the fish offal lying on the beaches and the salted cod drying on the flakes. Fortunately, it had been dissipated by the clean ocean winds before it could do more widespread damage or spread to other areas of the island. Still, before it had finally run its course, it devastated many families in the area.

For almost a week, Hannah Martin hovered on the brink of death, awakening but once or twice in that entire time-frame only to immediately lapse back into unconsciousness again. She lost so much weight that her already gaunt frame once again took on the skeletal appearance of her teenage years, and her tall thin body, alternating between periods of excessive sweating and paralyzing chills, curled itself into the fetal position of her birth as she slept.

When she regained consciousness on the sixth day, her fever finally broken, she found herself on her sleeping bench inside the hut covered with the woolen blanket that Father Fabian had given her. She had no recollection of how she had gotten there. She wondered how long she had been there.

Her first indication that she had finally returned to the land of the living, even before she opened her eyes for the first time in days, was the unmistakable aroma of rabbit stew permeating the interior of the hut. At first she thought she was only dreaming, but when she sat half upright on the bench, she saw through still blurred eyes that the pot from which the delicious aroma emanated sat on top of the coals that still glowed for a few seconds whenever a fresh puff of air passed over them.

Suddenly ravenously hungry, she wanted only to have some of the hot stew that tantalized her ten feet away in the center of the hut. By sheer force of will, she made herself get down from the sleeping bench and crawl to the fire where without pausing she greedily gulped down three or four mouthfuls of the most appetizing food she had eaten in years. Then, thirsty as well from her long ordeal, she drank some water from the pail that sat nearby and immediately knew by its cold freshness that it had only recently been fetched from the river.

And the following day, when she finally felt strong enough to venture outside, she saw that someone had collected a supply of dry dead-fall wood and stacked it neatly next to the hovel, ready for burning.

She wished that Father Fabian had been there at that moment so that she could thank him for his kindness. At the same time she was thankful that he couldn't see her in her woeful condition.

Over the space of the next three weeks she gradually regained her strength, recovered some of the weight that she had lost, and got her life back to some semblance of normality. By the end of that time she felt strong enough to begin to harvest the first of her new crop of potatoes. She wanted to make sure that she had them all properly cached before the onset of frost.

It was another week before Father Fabian paid his next visit. Hannah was extremely glad to see him and started to thank him profusely for his acts of kindness and compassion while she had been sick. Even as she spoke she knew by the puzzled look on his face that the young priest had no prior knowledge of anything that she was telling him.

When she explained, he told her, "It wasn't me, Hannah, for I've been sick myself for the past three weeks and have only just now gotten out of my own bed. I wasn't even able to bury some of the poor souls who died while I was ill."

Father Fabian was mystified by what Hannah had told him. Hannah herself, however, now knew with absolute certainty who had looked after her while she had been ill. A few days later she again had the feeling of being watched as she worked in her garden. This time she stood and saw the tall blond-haired man standing at the far edge of the clearing. He made no effort at concealment. She went to him and, for the first time since his mother had held him in her arms as a baby, Peter Kerrivan knew the wonder of a woman's embrace.

twentyone

Kerrivan, despite the hard life he had led and the brutality and violence that had surrounded him for most of his twenty-eight years, could not condone the senseless acts of destruction and savagery committed by Johnson, Foley, Shaheen, and Styles. Neither could Finn and the Shannahan brothers. The fact that they expected him to do something about it, although they hadn't said as much outright, bothered Kerrivan because he knew he was not fulfilling their expectations of him as the actions of the wayward men continued unchecked.

He was also concerned about what might eventually happen to himself and the other original members of the band if they were caught. The settlers and the authorities would have no way of differentiating between the men who had committed the atrocious acts and those who hadn't been involved. Although it was a moot point because he knew they would all be hanged in any event if captured, it was nevertheless important to him. He did not want to be cast in the same mold as Johnson and the others, even on the gallows.

He did not have any hold over the men, who only laughed in the face of his repeated attempts to try to get them to restrain their violent behavior. His only recourse, he concluded, short of killing them, was to try to mitigate the impact of their destruction as best he could by staying as close to them as possible when they were carrying out their raids into the settlements.

His greatest concern was for Hannah Martin. Having to pass by her hut in the clearing in the woods every time the band made a foray into Renews, he knew that if he himself were not present on every single occasion, Johnson and the other men would undoubtedly eventually be tempted to stop there to pay her a visit. When he told the men that he would kill anyone who went near the woman or laid a hand on her, they could see the seriousness of the threat in his piercing blue eyes, an understanding that was reinforced by the hulking Ned Finn who added, "And if Peter doesn't kill you, I will. I'll tear you apart with my bare hands, and I'll feed your mangy carcasses to the animals and the crows out on the moor."

Despite Kerrivan's attempts to curb the violent activities of Johnson, Styles, Foley, and Shaheen, the frequency and magnitude of their barbaric acts escalated. On most of their earlier raids, they had usually been contented to knock down a fence or two or to destroy some outbuilding before returning to the mountain. When that failed to continue to give them the warped satisfaction that they craved, they turned to arson – burning boats and fishing rooms, and, on one occasion, a house from which the sleeping occupants barely escaped with their lives. They killed livestock, desecrated churches and grave-yards, and afterwards, when they returned to the indentation in the cliff, got as much depraved pleasure out of the recounting of their violent acts as perhaps they had gotten out of committing them in the first place.

Kerrivan had been sickened, but not particularly surprised, to witness Johnson, on one such occasion, salivating as he described the atrocities he had inflicted upon a dog whose barking had interrupted his activities on a previous foray, before leaving it beheaded and disemboweled on the doorstep of the settler who owned it. Kerrivan could not reconcile the man's bizarre behavior to the fact that only a few minutes later, Johnson picked up his lute and treated them all to yet another beautifully played rendition of the ageless classic, Danny Boy, as if nothing had happened.

With the passage of time, matters got even worse. On a subsequent raid into Fermeuse, an unfortunate settler who happened to come upon Johnson and his cronies at the wrong moment, was beaten and left lying on the beach where the incoming tide came within inches of drowning him as he lay there unconscious. Fortunately, the man somehow escaped serious injury and within a day or two was back at his work. The incident, however, raised the specter of what was yet to come.

What had started as a nuisance to the five settlements on

this section of the coast three years earlier had, in the space of the few months since Johnson's arrival, escalated into a reign of terror that struck fear into the heart of every man, woman, and child in the area. Families were afraid to sleep at night, mothers were loath to let their children out of their sight, and men were reluctant to leave their wives and families alone for any length of time, even in broad daylight. They were all held at ransom in their own homes and communities, never knowing when or where the outlaws would strike next. Everyone from Ferryland to Cappahayden was convinced that it would be only a matter of time before someone was seriously hurt, or worse.

And, before the passing of another month, their worst fears were confirmed when early one morning the body of Thomas Murphy, a father of five young children, was found in a meadow a short distance from his house at the outer edge of the settlement. The back of his head had been crushed by a deathblow of extreme force. There was some evidence in the grass that he had put up a struggle against his assailants and had perhaps tried to make his way to his own door after they had left him there. While there was no direct proof to link anyone in the outlaw band to the killing, nobody in the area was prepared to accept any other possible explanation for the villainous deed.

For the people of the region, the death of Murphy was the occurrence that finally turned their fear and anxiety to rage. The men and women of the settlement of Renews, where Murphy had lived and which had itself continued to be the prime target of the outlaw band, were particularly incensed, and they descended en masse once again on Lieutenant Stanford in the garrison in the Ferryland Plantation, demanding that he take action and rid the area of the scourge that had plagued them for so long – once and for all.

twentytwo

Kerrivan was as appalled as everybody else by the senseless killing of Thomas Murphy. He had been with Finn and the Shannahan brothers in another part of Renews at the moment the murder was committed, in violation of his own resolution to stay close to Johnson and the others to keep an eye on them, and his first inkling that something had gone horribly wrong back in the settlement came when the band was halfway back to the Butterpot mountain.

Sensing Kerrivan's change in mood when he found out what had transpired, Johnson, suddenly wary about how Kerrivan and the others would react, looked to Foley, Shaheen, and Styles for support and affirmation as he tried to explain.

"We were only having a bit of fun with him. How were we supposed to know that he would try to take us all on?"

The satanic sneer on Johnson's face as he related what had happened only an hour earlier and his boldfaced boasting about his own role in the killing so infuriated Kerrivan that, for one of the very few times in his life, he lost control. Before Johnson could make any move to escape or defend himself, Kerrivan had him by the throat, choking him, crushing his larynx and windpipe as he struggled in vain to extricate himself from Kerrivan's iron grip.

None of the other men tried to intervene, either to side with Kerrivan in his moment of fury or to come to Johnson's rescue. They all watched and waited to see what the final outcome of the violent drama unfolding on the moonlit barrens would be. Kerrivan's blind rage left him as quickly as it had started, however, and when he came to his senses, he knew by the strangely mottled look of Johnson's face, the man's frantic gulps to suck oxygen back into his air-starved lungs, and the glaze of his blood-streaked eyes, that he had come within a second or two of committing murder himself.

Finn, who had been as outraged as Kerrivan by the murder of Murphy, was prepared to finish what Kerrivan had started. The knife that he habitually wore in his waistband had been transferred to his right hand during the struggle, ready to be used at the first indication that Foley, Shaheen, or Styles might decide to enter the fray. Only Kerrivan's urging held him back, and Kerrivan himself, his sanity restored, now realized that he could no longer put off doing something about Johnson and his companions. Maybe it was already too late. Maybe turning Finn loose on them was the answer after all.

Little did he know at that moment, as he turned and headed for the mountain, leaving the others in his wake, that within the course of the next three days his problem would be solved for him by the sequence of events that would begin to unfold when Murphy's lifeless body was discovered early the next morning.

Lieutenant Stanford's first reaction when he saw the mob of settlers milling around the grounds of the garrison had been to send them home again, a task that he delegated to the two officers he sent out to talk to them. Having been apprised of the details of the murder earlier that morning, he knew the purpose of the settlers' unannounced visit and had no desire to meet with them himself.

In their determination to see Murphy's death avenged and the safety and sanctity of their own troubled homes and communities restored, the settlers would neither leave nor be deterred in their efforts to speak to the Lieutenant of the garrison, the one person with the ultimate responsibility to see that justice was served and that Murphy's killers were caught and hanged.

When his officers returned, they told him, "Sir, they won't talk to us. They say they'll stay there until they can talk to you directly, and that they'll fire the garrison if you don't come out. With all due respect, Sir, I think you should meet with them. I've never seen them this angry before. There must be a hundred of them, with more coming every minute."

Stanford, with little other choice, finally went out to meet with the settlers, and when he did he saw in their eyes and their faces a fire and a determination that he hadn't witnessed in any of their previous encounters. When they spoke, he instinctively gauged the depth and intensity of their rage and the seriousness of their threat to burn the garrison to the ground if he didn't do something. He also knew that if the settlers, all men hardened like his own soldiers by the harsh environment in which they existed, took it upon themselves to rise up en masse against him, he and his men would be hard-pressed to keep them in check.

So, for the ninth time in three years, he mobilized his forces for yet another venture into the wilderness. This time he sent all but a handful of his men, leaving the prisoners and most of the indentured men and women of the garrison confined under lock and key to ensure that they would still be there when they returned. The normal functioning of the garrison could wait. He also permitted, for the first time, a number of the disgruntled settlers to accompany his men. Before letting them go, he made it abundantly clear what he expected of them, and then retired to the refuge of the garrison dining room to pour himself tumbler after tumbler of stiff Irish whiskey while he waited.

He didn't have to wait long. Incredibly, only a few hours later, just as he was rousing himself from a liquor induced nap on the couch, his men returned, bringing with them, to his utter amazement, two of the outlaws – Styles and none other than the murderer himself, Nate Johnson.

He couldn't believe it. Even when his officers told him the strange circumstances under which they had apprehended the two men, he didn't care. He had what he wanted, two of the outlaws who he was sure would bring him Kerrivan and the others, and perhaps even more importantly, bring about his recall to England.

He couldn't have picked a more perfect time to have initiated the search. On the previous night, Johnson, Styles, Foley, and Shaheen had been unable to resist the temptation to sneak back into the settlement of Renews to see firsthand the aftermath of their bloody handiwork. While there, they had relieved one of the settlers of a half-filled keg of dark rum that they took with them when they left again for the mountain. As they made their way across the barrens, the men had taken turns with the keg and were all intoxicated before they were even halfway across. With two miles left to go, they stopped to rest for a while, continuing to pass around the potent liquor as they sat on the ground.

The stop that had been intended to be only a few minutes stretched into a few hours, and when Foley and Shaheen finally arose and groped their way toward the mountain, they left Johnson and Styles behind, sleeping like children in the alders. And that was how Stanford's men found them the next morning, the empty rum keg lying on its side a few feet away.

When Stanford saw Johnson and Styles for the first time, he couldn't quite accept the fact that these were two of the men that had kept him and his soldiers at bay for more than three years. Johnson, he quickly realized, would be of no use to him, for when the two fugitives had awakened on the barrens to find themselves surrounded by an army of soldiers and settlers, Johnson's drunken reaction had been to lash out at his captors and to try to make a run for it. He received for his efforts a blow to the head that rendered him senseless, a condition from which he would never again emerge. Styles, who realized immediately that the game was up, had shown no resistance and had meekly surrendered himself into the hands of Stanford's men.

In Styles, Stanford saw only the wretched shell of a man who reeked of urine, vomit, alcohol and accumulated dirt and grime that had covered his unwashed body for months. He was unable to accept the reality that this miserable creature was someone who had outsmarted and eluded him at every turn for such a long time. But it didn't matter. Whatever his appearance and level of intelligence, he was confident that the dissipated excuse for manhood that he was looking at was the means through which Kerrivan and the other members of the outlaw band would be delivered into his hands before the day was done. And, while he didn't realize it at the time, he could have had none better in his custody than Styles, the Snitch, whose life had been an endless succession of betrayal of his fellow man.

"Well, well, well, my fine fellow, we meet at last. And the funny part is that I don't even know which one you are – or him," indicating the semi-conscious Johnson. Styles, having supplied the information that Stanford had requested and knowing what was coming next, threw out his one and only gambit.

"What will it mean to me if I take you to Kerrivan and the others?"

Styles's question caught Stanford off guard. On many prior occasions he had witnessed the misguided loyalty that criminals often have for each other, and had expected that it would take some time, perhaps even a measure of torture, to extract the end result that Styles had so freely offered. He didn't know that it was Johnson who had actually committed the murder. It wouldn't have mattered in any case. In Stanford's mind the slaying of Thomas Murphy was a collective act of the entire outlaw band, and they would all pay the same price for their evil deed.

"I can't spare your life, it's gone much too far for that. You know that as well as I do. But if Kerrivan is in my hands by sunset, I'll see that you die a quick death by gunfire, and you won't have to face the gallows."

And Styles, who had spent his entire adult life in mortal fear of one day feeling a noose around his neck and who was now reconciled to the fact that there was no way out, opted for the lesser of the two evils and made his own pact with the devil to offer up the men with whom he had lived for the last four years.

Within the hour, Stanford's men were again headed in the direction of the Butterpot mountain with Stanford, unable to resist the desire to be there when Kerrivan and his men were finally cornered, himself now leading the way. This was a moment that he had dreamed about and looked forward to for three long, miserable years.

As they progressed toward their destination, Styles thought about the abuse and mistreatment that he had received from the other members of the outlaw band. Despite his own impending doom, he felt the sweet satisfaction of knowing that when he went, he would take Kerrivan and the others with him. He hated them all, the Shannahan brothers, Foley and Shaheen, his own partners in crime, even the two young Irish boys – Kerrivan most of all.

But when he thought about Finn, the man who had at one time almost strangled him to death, he could only remember awakening in the indentation in the cliff to feel his own frozen body in the embrace of Finn's huge arms, and seeing the compassion and caring in the big man's eyes, and he knew that he could not betray the man who had bestowed upon him the only true act of kindness and humanity that he had ever known. With less than a mile to go the outlaws' lair, the tiny ember of decency that had lain dormant somewhere deep within Style's being all these years flickered into life, and he led Stanford and his men on a course that would take them to the northern side of the Butterpot mountain, well clear of the outlaws' hideout.

When Stanford realized that he, like his officers before him, had been duped, he erupted in rage and struck Styles across the face with his open palm. To Styles, for whom the slap in the face was not the first he had ever received, Stanford suddenly represented the sum total of all the oppression, deprivation, hardship, and abuse that he had known in his lifetime, and he spit directly into the Lieutenant's arrogant, beet-red face.

Stanford recoiled as if shot, and in a moment of insane anger made the decision that he would leave the capture of Kerrivan and the other members of the outlaw band for another day. All he wanted at that moment was to see Styles dangling on the end of a rope.

Despite the lateness of the afternoon, he ordered his men to build a makeshift gallows, not in the garrison compound where such executions were normally carried out, but in the centre of Ferryland where every man, woman and child in the plantation could witness the hanging that very day. Through this action they would know that he, Lieutenant Stanford, would make true on his commitment to the people of the area to hunt the outlaws to the ends of the earth if he had to.

It was almost nightfall before the hastily erected platform was finished and the hangings could commence. Stanford first had Johnson brought out and propped up by his men as the noose was placed over his head. Within a matter of seconds, without any of the ceremony and ritual that usually accompanied such occurrences, the murderer of Thomas Murphy was dispatched. Ironically, in his state of semi-consciousness, the man who had inflicted so much pain on others for such a long time, himself died a quick and relatively painless death.

Stanford had saved Styles for last. Repeated scrubbing had failed to remove the dirty feeling of Style's spit on his face, and he had taken three full-strength drinks from the whiskey decanter to steel himself before making his way to the site of the execution.

The day was nearing its end. The brilliance of the setting sun promised a fine tomorrow as Styles, oblivious to the jeers, taunts, and cheering of the crowd, climbed the steps of the gallows, feeling strangely calm and more content with himself than he had in a long, long time. As the noose was being fitted around his neck, the garrison chaplain offered him his last chance to repent and seek God's forgiveness for the sins that had placed him there. Styles, unrepentant to the end but having made his own peace of sorts with his Maker and with himself out in the wilderness hours earlier, told the chaplain to, "go to hell, you're no better than the rest of them."

And with those last words, Styles, the Snitch, plunged into a world of eternal darkness that he hoped would be kinder to him than his thirty-four years on earth had been.

twentythree

When Johnson and Styles didn't return to the hideout, Kerrivan made the assumption that they had been captured and took himself and the other members of the band further out into the wilderness to the west of the mountain. There was no doubt in his mind that with Johnson and Styles in custody, Stanford would waste very little time in coming after the rest of them. Finn had argued in favor of staying and making a stand on the mountain but Kerrivan convinced the rest of the men otherwise, knowing that even though there were still eight of them if he included Foley, Shaheen and the two Irish boys in addition to the Shannahan brothers, they would be no match for the firepower that Stanford could bring to bear against them. He had also briefly considered moving to one of the band's alternate hideout locations on the southern or western side of the mountain. He knew, however, that Styles and Johnson would be sure to lead Stanford and his men there too when they found the indentation in the cliff deserted.

In the hastiness of their retreat, the men were able to take with them only a few items that they deemed essential to their survival out in the open wilderness – an axe, a little food, the means for catching trout and snaring rabbits and other small game, and the clothes that they wore on their backs. Everything else they left behind, out of sight inside the indentation in the cliff. They had no idea how long they might have to stay out there. Perhaps they might never be able to return to the relative comfort of the lair that had been their home for almost four years. And to make matters worse, the weather was already growing colder with the arrival of fall.

The person who had been their only friend and ally in the

entire area, Father Fabian O'Donnell, was shocked and bitterly disappointed to learn of the murder of Thomas Murphy, whom he had known to be a God-fearing man and a good provider for his family. The sense of betrayal he felt when he first heard the news caused him to wonder for the first time if, through his own continuing surreptitious acts of kindness toward the men in the wilderness, he had somehow unwittingly abetted them in the killing. Maybe, he reasoned, without his regular contributions to their welfare, they might have long since moved on to some other place. Perhaps in retrospect he should have paid more heed to the feeling of guilt that he had experienced each time he had tried to help the outlaws – or Hannah Martin, the recluse in the woods, for that matter.

He hadn't been present in Ferryland for the hanging of Johnson and Styles. It had all happened so quickly that he, like most of the people of the other settlements in the area, had not found out about the executions until the following day. Even though the executions had taken place outside his own parish, Father Fabian was deeply disturbed by the fact that the two men had not been buried with the full rites of the Roman Catholic Church to which they were entitled, convicted criminals or otherwise. Instead, Stanford had ordered that their weighted bodies be taken a short distance outside of the Ferryland Harbor immediately after the hangings and dumped into the sea. Nor, or so he was told, had either of the two Roman Catholic priests of the Ferryland Parish participated in any way in the final moments of the two executed men. They had merely been spectators in the crowd.

News of the hanging of Johnson and Styles spread along the coast like wildfire. Only Hannah Martin in her isolation in the clearing in the woods had not heard about the killing until Father Fabian visited her a few weeks later and told her about it. She too was shocked by the news. She couldn't in her own mind reconcile the murder of Murphy, although she didn't know him, with her own feelings toward Peter Kerrivan. Since her first face to face emotional encounter with him following her illness, Kerrivan had visited her on several subsequent occasions, showing up at random when she least expected him, sometimes staying all night. In that time she had come to believe that despite the fact that he was a wanted outlaw living in the wilderness, he was at heart a caring and decent man, driven there by circumstances beyond his control. Now she was no longer certain.

Lieutenant Stanford, like Father Fabian and Hannah Martin, was also troubled. Not by any feelings of concern for the welfare of Kerrivan and the other members of the outlaw band, but by the realization that in his rage and haste to hang Johnson and Styles, he had wasted the larger and more important opportunity to capture them all. He now feared that his intemperate course of action that day might now delay his recall to England a little longer than he had hoped for.

Still, in trying to put the best face on what in retrospect had clearly been a bad decision, he composed an account of the capture and execution of the two outlaws and forwarded it to his superiors in England on an eastbound fishing vessel. In it, he again provided an exaggerated version of what had actually taken place and gave his full assurance that by his actions he had effectively put a stop to the activities of the rest of the outlaws and had restored peace and tranquility to the area. Instead of including the broad hints and cleverly constructed phrases that had marked most of his previous dispatches, this time he made an outright request for recall. Perhaps, he hoped, he hadn't blown his chances of reassignment after all. He would simply have to wait and see.

It would be almost a month before Kerrivan and the other members of the band were able to go back to the indentation in the cliff. Their stay in the western wilderness had been a return to the manner of living of their initial days at the base of the Butterpot mountain, scouring the barrens for food by day, and sleeping at night in the open or in the shelter of some copse of trees or alders, trying to keep themselves warm and dry as best they could by covering themselves with boughs and leaves.

It was a difficult period for them all, especially the now subdued Foley and Shaheen, whose ability to fend for themselves was minimal at best. Although removed from the influence of Johnson and Styles, the two men still kept to themselves as much as possible, taking care to avoid angering either Kerrivan or Finn, having seen what both men were capable of doing when enraged. The Shannahan brothers, as usual, did their best to make the most of whatever circumstances they found themselves in. For Brian Duffy and Paddy O'Brien, however, the exile in the wilderness was just another chapter in their continuing grand adventure with the outlaw band.

In their four week period away from the Butterpot, Kerrivan and Finn made a number of trips back to the mountain, always under the cover of darkness. On none of these occasions had they seen any sign of Stanford's men or anyone else, yet each time they decided to wait a little longer until they were certain that it was safe for them to return. When they eventually did go back, Kerrivan was amazed that there was no indication anywhere that the indentation in the cliff had been disturbed in any manner. Everything was exactly as they had left it. It would be almost another full year before he and the other members of the band would find out the truth of what had taken place – that Styles had not betrayed them after all, and that the man whom they had all despised and abused had gone to his death taking with him the secret of the location of their hiding place at the base of the mountain.

twentyfour

The five-month period following the hanging of Johnson and Styles was one of peace and tranquility for the settlements of Ferryland, Aquaforte, Fermeuse, Renews, and Cappahayden, all of which had been plagued in varying degrees by the outlaw band for four years. Life for the settlers gradually returned to normal and many believed that they had finally seen the last of Kerrivan and his men.

The first snow of winter fell in early December, two months after the hangings and a few weeks earlier than usual, and the winter and early spring of 1755 passed with no indication that the outlaws were still anywhere within the area. Most people believed they had fled to St. John's or somewhere further into the interior. They began to relax and turned their time and attention to the full-time effort of eking out an existence in the harsh environment in which they lived. They could do without the distraction of the outlaw band.

It wasn't until the middle of March, when a new round of thefts was reported from Ferryland to Cappahayden, that the settlers knew that the outlaws were back. They couldn't believe it. What would it take to make them go away? Two of their numbers had been caught and hanged. Yet the rest were still out there, carrying on their raids again as if nothing had happened. Discouraged, the residents of the five affected settlements called upon Lieutenant Stanford once more to renew his efforts to find and apprehend them.

The raids of the outlaws continued unabated into the summer. They struck at random with no discernable pattern that could give the settlers or the authorities any idea of where they might hit next. In all this time, however, there was no further violence or wanton destruction. That, at least, brought the settlers a small measure of cold comfort.

Hannah Martin, as usual, had heard very little about what was taking place. The few bits of information and news that she had gotten over the past several months had been gleaned from her brief conversations with Father Fabian, who had come to see her three times since the hangings. On his first visit, a week or so after the executions had taken place, he told her the news. It was the first time she had heard anything about it. He had come again during the Christmas period, and again in late February to check to see how she was managing to get through the winter. She could tell by the sadness in his voice that he was as disappointed and as hurt as she had been at having his trust in Kerrivan and the other members of the outlaw band so badly betrayed.

Her first indication that Kerrivan was back came in mid-June while she was kneeling on the mossy bank of Peter's Brook washing her hair in the cool flowing stream and she saw his reflection in the water. Even though his features were distorted by the movement of the water, she knew it was him. She didn't rise or turn around. The long shudder that went through her body rooted her to the ground. She didn't know what to do or say.

"Hello Hannah."

The richness of his voice brought back the memories of their times together in the clearing in the woods. She was powerless to move. She didn't resist when he reached down to take her by her shoulders and gently lift her to her feet. She mutely followed him back to the clearing, where he first sat her on the soft grass before settling himself down beside her. And then he told her everything that had happened, all of it, omitting nothing, even his own negligence on the night that Murphy had been murdered.

When she knew the truth of all that had transpired, relief washed over her and the tears that she had been desperately trying to hold back burst forth, wetting her face and blurring her vision. And when Kerrivan held her in his arms again, she knew that her love for him was deep and true and that she would never doubt him again, no matter what the future might bring.

A few days later Father Fabian paid her another visit. When she told him about Kerrivan's reappearance and what he had told her, he was as relieved as she had been. That very same afternoon, for the first time in many months, he walked without any feeling of guilt halfway to the Butterpot mountain with his white flag, renewing his pledge to himself to try to offer what little comfort he could to the wild men in the wilderness.

The rest of that summer was relatively uneventful. Even though the raids of the outlaws persisted, the settlers no longer felt the same level of fear and dread that had existed at the height of Johnson's, Shaheen's, and Foley's reign of terror. The fact that they continued to lose things to the outlaws, despite their best efforts to protect them, still bothered and angered them. But the existence of the outlaws was now once again reduced to nothing more than an aggravating nuisance, not a matter of life and death.

During the months that followed, three more men came to join Kerrivan's band in the wilderness. The first one, an escaped convict named Gilbert Stacey, came alone. He wandered around for several days in the vicinity of the Butterpot mountain before the outlaws finally saw fit to take him in. The other two arrived together. Their attempt to burglarize the home of a wealthy merchant in St. John's had been their first and only criminal initiative. When their intrusion into the darkened mansion had been detected, they had managed to elude their pursuers and fled from the city to make their way to the Southern Shore and eventually into the outlaw band. The pair, a Welshman named Silas Woodford, and his partner in crime, a deaf mute named Alfred Barron, was, in Kerrivan's estimation, an odd and unlikely alliance. It was obvious to him and the others that the childlike Barron had been led down the pathway of crime by the older and craftier Woodford.

Kerrivan, because of his bitter experience with Johnson, Shaheen, and Foley, was anxious to know what the three newcomers were really like before he committed himself. He didn't want any more of Johnson's kind. Although it would be some time before he trusted any of the new men enough to permit them to accompany him and the other members of the band on their forays into the settlements, his fears would eventually prove to be unfounded. The three newcomers fitted in well and Kerrivan's concerns were gradually dispelled. Woodford, despite his Welsh origins, struck up an instant friendship with the Irish Shannahan brothers – and in Barron, Brian Duffy and Paddy O'Brien had a new companion.

twentyfive

James Kilfoy was not a well-liked man – and he didn't know why. Indeed, if the many people in the area who disliked him were asked why that was the case, the vast majority of them would be hard-pressed to point to any specific thing that caused them to feel as they did toward him. Kilfoy was, unfortunately, one of those individuals whose combination of looks, personality, and mannerisms made people feel uncomfortable and ill at ease in his presence, and they simply avoided him whenever they could.

He couldn't understand it. He was as honest and trustworthy as the next man, kept himself cleaner and more presentable than most other men in the settlement, tried to be friendly to everyone he met, and had never done anything that he could remember to harm anyone in the area.

He was now thirty-one years of age and still wifeless. Despite the fact that he had a house of his own and knew that he would be a good provider, the few liaisons that he had had with women during the past fifteen years had all ended almost as soon as they had begun. It was never by his choice and he was never given any explanation that he could understand or accept. And as time passed, he became lonelier and increasingly unhappy with his lot in life. He often thought about moving to some other part of Newfoundland, perhaps St. John's, where he might be able to fit in more easily and start over.

Today, however, he felt better than he had in a long time. He had a secret – one that, if he played his cards right, might finally earn him the recognition and respect that he craved. And one that should gain him a few shillings in the bargain. Tomorrow morning he would go to Ferryland to see Lieutenant Stanford and set his plan in motion.

Stanford was finishing his breakfast when he was told that a settler from Fermeuse was asking to see him and that the man said he had something very important to tell him, something that Lieutenant Stanford would be pleased to hear.

Stanford was in a foul mood. "Send him away. I don't want to see anyone this morning, especially some ignorant lout who has nothing better to do than waste my time and his own."

Stanford was still smarting from the reply he had received only a few weeks earlier to the dispatch he had sent to his superiors in England after the hanging of Styles and Johnson. He had been passed the white envelope bearing the seal of His Majesty's Royal Navy by the captain of a visiting naval ship whom he was entertaining for the evening. He had placed it inside his uniform jacket, confident that it contained the recall notice he had requested. During the rest of the evening his thoughts were as much on the letter next to his chest as they were on the social event that he was hosting. He longed for everyone to leave so that he could read it in private.

Finally, well after midnight, he found himself alone in the garrison dining room. After pouring himself a tumbler of Irish whiskey, a welcomed departure from the port wine he had been drinking for most of the evening as a courtesy to his guests, he settled himself in his chair, pulled off his boots, and drew the letter from his jacket – and couldn't believe what he read:

"... commended for your success in capturing and bringing to justice the outlaws Styles and Johnson. Hopefully you are correct in your assumption that your actions have restored peace and order to the area. You are encouraged to take all further steps to capture the remaining fugitives and ..."

Enraged, he hurled the whiskey glass against the wall, smashing it to bits, and crumpled the letter into a ball before throwing it into the open flames of the fireplace. He hadn't even bothered to read the rest of it. The letter had made no reference at all to his request for reassignment. It had been ignored and he was frustrated yet again in his efforts to get away from this miserable, God-forsaken place that he hated so much.

And this morning his head throbbed and his tongue felt like

rough leather in his mouth. Neither the breakfast of bacon and eggs nor the shot of whiskey, 'the hair of the dog,' he had taken had done much to alleviate his hangover, a situation that had been repeated almost every morning since the letter arrived. And what, if anything, could some loutish settler possibly have to tell him that was of any importance anyway?

Yet, as he turned away to settle himself in for another morning alone in the garrison's dining room, some instinct made him tell his aide to go back to the man and ask him what it was that he wanted to say. Seconds later, the aide returned relaying Kilfoy's message that he could deliver the remaining outlaws in the wilderness into Stanford's hands if given the chance.

When Kilfoy was ushered in, Stanford could barely contain his disdain and contempt. Kilfoy was the type of man who epitomized the uncivilized, uncultured, primitive environment in which he had wasted more than a dozen years of his life.

"My good man, this had better be good. If not, you'll be sorry that you came here this morning – that I can guarantee you."

"Lieutenant Stanford, sir, I've only come here to do my duty to the King. I've no other motive, I can assure you, than to help you bring Kerrivan and the other outlaws to justice."

"And how, my fine fellow, do you propose to do that when all others have failed?" Stanford's skepticism showed clearly on his bloated face.

Kilfoy was not deterred. "Well, sir, it's like this. Do you know Father O'Donnell, the priest in Renews? He's been secretly helping the outlaws all these years without anyone knowing about it. I know it for a fact. I've seen him doing it. Every month or so, he leaves a bundle of stuff, food I suppose, for them in a large tree at the edge of the barrens. By some sort of signal, as far as I can figure it, the outlaws always come to claim it when the coast is clear."

"How do you know this?" Stanford was suddenly attentive.

Kilfoy, encouraged by Stanford's new interest, continued, "I happened to be on the barrens myself one day when I saw it all happen. After that I kept an eye on the good Father almost every day to see if he would do it again. And he did, three times in three months. So, as I see it, if you watch Father O'Donnell, sooner or later he will deliver them right into your hands without even knowing that he's doing it."

Kilfoy felt the bloodshot eyes of Stanford burning into him and read their unmistakable message that if things were not as he was saying, it would be he himself who would be in serious trouble. For a moment or two he almost regretted coming. But his belief that he would be the acclaimed instrument through which the outlaws would finally be brought to justice overrode his fear of Stanford, and he assured the Lieutenant of the garrison that, "What I told you is the gospel truth. You can count on that, sir. And what about the reward, the ten shillings?"

"You'll get your ten shillings when I get Kerrivan and the others. And if what you told me is a pack of lies, I'll see that you get something else. And you can count on that. Now get out of here."

From the dining room window, Stanford watched Kilfoy's departing figure until the man exited through the garrison gate. After pouring himself another whiskey, he stood for an extended period of time staring into the fire mulling over what Kilfoy had told him. Perhaps, he thought, it wasn't too late after all.

twentysix

Their first few days back in their mountain hideaway made the outlaws appreciate it's warmth and comfort all the more. Once again they slept dry at night, sheltered from the elements, and had a ready supply of food all around them. The air of depression and desperation that had pervaded their stay in the western-most reaches of the wilderness area quickly lifted, and their everyday existence soon reverted to its previous comfortable pattern. The vast bulk of the mountain itself lent comfort and cheer, and gave them the reassurance that they were once again safe and secure within its familiar confines. Even the dour attitudes of Foley and Shaheen improved a little, prompting Kerrivan to think that without Johnson around to influence them, the two men might yet reach the point where they could at least get along a little better with the other members of the band.

Kerrivan reinstated the band's system of watch-keeping in case Stanford and his men should come looking for them again. Now, for the first time, he included Foley and Shaheen in the rotation, as well as Duffy and O'Brien. Prior to this, he had never had enough faith in Foley or Shaheen to entrust the safety and well-being of himself and the other members of the band into their hands, and he had deemed the boys too young and inexperienced for the responsibility that watch duty entailed. Having now reconsidered, he decided to let Foley and Shaheen stand watch individually, but felt compelled to make the boys stand watch together to lessen the likelihood that one or the other of them would fall asleep while on duty.

It was during the boys' turn, two months after their return to the mountain, that Kerrivan, who had himself kept the previous night's watch, was awakened by Paddy O'Brien's excited shout, "Peter. Come quick. The priest is out there again with his white flag."

It was the first time in several months that Father Fabian had tried to make contact with them. Kerrivan had correctly assumed that the young priest had given up on them because of Murphy's murder and all that had ensued in its aftermath. When he had visited Hannah Martin a few weeks earlier and told her what had really happened, she had confided to him that, "I'm sure Father Fabian will be just as happy as I am to know the rights of it all." He himself at the time had felt as if a great load had been lifted from his shoulders when he unburdened himself to Hannah and knew by her response that she had believed him and accepted the truth of what had occurred.

"Can me and Brian go to see what he's left this time?" O'Brien pleaded.

Although the priest's packages had always contained items of the most basic nature, usually bits of food and occasional items of clothing or mundane but practical objects like fishhooks and sulfur matches, the anticipation of finding out what was inside the next package was always an exciting diversion for the two boys. Never having had much in the way of personal possessions at any time in their lives, they were never disappointed by anything that the package contained, or did not. On the one occasion that Father Fabian had included a book, they had both been ecstatic. Even though neither of them could read more than a few simple words, the pictures in the book had kept them enthralled for hours. Especially the one showing a single man, armed only with a longbow, fending off a virtual army of mail-clad enemies. Somehow, the picture struck close to home.

Kerrivan decided that this time he would delegate the trip across the barrens to the Fairy Tree to Foley and Shaheen. Some instinct told him not to send the boys. Their disappointment showed plainly on their faces, but he resisted their pleas and entreaties until they finally gave up and left him alone. Besides, he reasoned, it would be an opportunity for Foley and Shaheen to begin to earn their keep.

The two men were as startled and surprised as Finn and the others when Kerrivan asked them to retrieve the package.

They would have preferred to stay where they were and avoid having to make the arduous trek across the barrens and back, a total distance of almost five miles. Still, they made no protest, perhaps realizing that this might be a chance for them to improve their relationship with the other members of the band, which to this point had been tenuous at best. The thought may have also crossed their minds that perhaps there might be something in the package that they could claim for themselves or consume without the others being aware of it.

Foley and Shaheen were no more than a quarter of a mile in the distance when Brian Duffy and Paddy O'Brien made the conscious decision to follow them, an act of disobedience that would have grave consequences for themselves and the entire outlaw band. It was the first time they had ever blatantly disobeyed any order that Kerrivan or Finn had given them. Usually they did whatever they were told without question, knowing that they would most likely receive a good cuffing or worse if they didn't. This time, however, the lure of the package in the tree, with the promise that it might contain another book or perhaps something even better, was too much for them to resist.

Keeping well behind Foley and Shaheen, avoiding detection by keeping to the wales and the alders, they trailed the two men across the open barrens. Their concern about what Kerrivan would do to them when they returned was all but forgotten for the moment. At one point they were sure that they had been spotted, but when neither Foley nor Shaheen turned back to confront them, they continued on, keeping a safe distance as they followed. Their only wish was that the two men ahead of them would walk a little faster.

It took them fifty minutes to cross the barrens. Duffy and O'Brien were only a hundred yards behind when Foley and Shaheen reached the tree and stood under its spreading foliage. Making no further effort to conceal their presence, safe in the knowledge that the two men would not send them back now anyway, they sprinted the rest of the way to join them. They wanted to be there on the spot when the package was lifted down from the tree.

Unfortunately, neither Duffy nor O'Brien ever got to see

what Father Fabian's package of kindness contained. Nor did Foley or Shaheen, or any of the other members of the outlaw band for that matter. Before the package was fetched from its perch in the tree, the two men and the two boys were suddenly surrounded by soldiers and settlers who materialized without warning out of the woods and the bushes. There was no escape. Within seconds they were bound hand and foot, scarcely able to grasp the undeniable reality that they had been captured.

Stanford recognized Duffy and O'Brien at once. He was surprised to see them there, having assumed that they had long since left the area, if not Newfoundland. He didn't know who the other two were, only that they were not Kerrivan, Finn, or the Shannahan brothers. It hardly mattered. With these four in his grasp, he would surely now find out where Kerrivan and the rest of the outlaws were hiding.

It took only a few minutes of soldierly persuasion to get Foley and Shaheen to agree to lead him and his men back across the barrens to the place where the other members of the outlaw band would be awaiting their return. This time there would be no blind trails or tricks. He would see to that by dividing his contingent of men and settlers into two groups, placing one of the outlaws in each party. They would approach the mountain from slightly different directions. With Foley and Shaheen now parted and unable to communicate with each other, Stanford would know immediately if he was being fooled once again if he saw at any time that both parties were not converging on exactly the same spot in the distance. Duffy and O'Brien were left behind in the custody of two of his soldiers.

The two outlaws led their respective groups straight to the indentation in the cliff. Despite the speed with which Stanford and his men had crossed the barrens, Kerrivan and the other members of the outlaw band were not there when they arrived. The obviously lived-in appearance of the lair told Stanford that neither Foley nor Shaheen had lied or tried to trick him. Still, he was furious that his main quarry had eluded him yet again. Foley, realizing the seriousness of his own situation, made a desperate attempt to curry favor with his captors by telling him about the outlaws' alternate hiding places and volunteering to lead him there. But these places too proved to be deserted.

twenty-six

Once again Kerrivan and the other outlaws had melted into the vast sweep of the western wilderness.

Stanford knew that it would be futile to proceed any further at that time. Contented for the moment with what he had, he and his men retraced their steps back to the Fairy Tree, where they collected Duffy, O'Brien, and the remaining two soldiers and made their way back to the Ferryland Plantation. Although he was still angry and frustrated about missing Kerrivan, Finn, the Shannahan brothers, and whoever else might now be in the band, he felt better than he had in a very long time. He would dispatch the four outlaws now in his custody in due course, and come back at another time for the rest of them. A whiskey or two back in the garrison would round out a productive day.

twentyseven

T he hangings were set for noon on May 29th to allow ample time for everyone in the surrounding area to be informed and be able to attend. It was, ironically, the anniversary of the arrival of the first of the outlaws, Kerrivan, Finn, and Styles, four years earlier. Stanford realized now that the earlier executions of Johnson and Styles had been carried out too hastily. Only the people who had been in Ferryland at the time had been able to witness them, while the vast majority of the settlers of Renews, Aquaforte, Fermeuse, and Cappahayden had only heard about it after the fact. Thus, for Stanford, a good opportunity to promote himself in a better light had been squandered. This time he wanted every man, woman, and child within a fifty-mile radius to be able to come and see the four captured outlaws get their just desserts. And know that it was he who had brought them to heel.

This time, too, he decided to change the venue of the hangings from Ferryland to Renews, where the greatest impact of the outlaw band had been felt over the years. In preparation for the event, he sent his men there well ahead of time to erect the gallows, knowing that its ominous presence in the community for all to see would heighten the settlers' senses for the occasion.

By 8:00 a.m. on the day of the hangings, a crowd had already gathered on the beach of Renews where the executions were to take place. Even at that early hour, long before the outlaws themselves would arrive and be led up onto the platform, there was already an air of jollity and celebration in the settlement. Fathers and mothers brought their young sons and daughters with them so that they too could witness and remember the events of that momentous day. Some even brought food and drink, making it a family outing.

As if by prearrangement, even the weather was cooperating. The damp fog and drizzle that had marked the previous three days had lifted and blue sky stretched from horizon to horizon. As the hours passed, the temperature rose to a comfortable level, and the southwest wind that had been brisk earlier in the morning by 10:00 a.m. had moderated to a gentle, caressing breeze. Many men shed their coats and jackets as they smoked their pipes, passed jugs between them, and gambled and played cards while they waited. The laughter and screams of children filled the air as they played games and chased each other around the gallows. Women from the many settlements in the area gathered in small groups, exchanging news and gossip, enjoying a rare moment of socializing away from the toil and drudgery of their everyday existence. Others kept arriving every few minutes. Although the main event was still two hours away, it was already a festive occasion.

Finally, at 12:30 p.m., Stanford and his entourage arrived, slightly behind schedule. The journey from Ferryland had taken a little longer than anticipated. The four condemned outlaws were brought along in chains, escorted by a detail of guards dressed in their regimental best for the event. A slow drum roll told everybody that the proceedings were about to begin.

Gabriel Foley was the first of the outlaws to be led up the steps of the gallows. Dirty, unshaven, his clothes in tatters, he was only a shell of the man captured two weeks earlier. Bewildered, he seemed hardly aware of what was happening around him and looked as if he were wondering what he was doing there. He appeared to shrink into himself as the crowd hooted with glee and derision. He scarcely heard the garrison chaplain praying for his soon-to-be-departed soul.

"What are you going to do now, you filthy bugger?" The foghorn voice from somewhere in the crowd brought raucous laughter.

"Can't you just feel the rope around your neck, Foley? I hope it tears your bloody head from your body."

Someone else offered, "We'll pass it around and have a game of kickball with it."

More laughter and hilarity followed when a shrill voice, a

woman's, added, "And afterwards we'll feed it to the gulls. They'll fight over your eyeballs."

Others joined in to torment the condemned outlaw in his last moments. Some men hoisted their children up onto their shoulders so that they wouldn't miss anything. When the trio of women standing nearest to the gallows pointed at Foley as they convulsed with laughter, he didn't realize that it was because he had just urinated over the front of his trousers for all to see. And the same three women, like everybody else present, cheered loudly and lustily a few minutes later when the trap door dropped and Foley plunged to his death. His death was instant. The sound of his neck snapping was lost in the din of the moment.

Next came William Shaheen, every bit as terrified as Foley had been. Still, he glared defiantly at the crowd that taunted him as they tried their best to make his final moments on earth as miserable as possible, and ignored the chaplain's prayers and entreaties, refusing his last chance for atonement. And when the trapdoor opened for the second time, the crowd cheered even louder and longer. Shaheen's death was not clean. Unlike Foley, he took several minutes to die as he slowly strangled on the end of the rope. Even the grotesque convulsions of his suspended body did little to deflate the high spirits of the onlookers. They had waited a long time for this day.

When Shaheen's body had been taken aside and placed beside Foley's, the other two outlaws, Brian Duffy and Paddy O'Brien, were led forward. Suddenly, the crowd grew quiet. For the vast majority of them, it was the first time that they had seen either Duffy or O'Brien. The shock of seeing the two youths, not grown men like Foley and Shaheen, was something for which they were not prepared. It was not what they had expected.

"You can't hang them. They're just lads." It was the same foghorn voice that only minutes earlier had so lustily scorned and ridiculed Foley and Shaheen.

"Flog them. Put them in jail. Anything else. But not this. They're too young."

The mood of the crowd had changed. Their gaiety and jubilation were now replaced with concern and revulsion at what they were about to witness.

Stanford, taken aback by the crowd's reaction, hesitated. Although their mood had not yet escalated into outright anger, he himself was now concerned, not about the fate of the two boys, but by the fact that he had seen on two or three previous occasions the lengths to which an aroused mob could go when provoked. For a few minutes, he considered their obvious wish to cancel the rest of the hangings. But then he remembered that these two boys, despite their age, were every bit as responsible for his torturous overstay in Ferryland as Foley and Shaheen, or even Kerrivan, Finn, and the Shannahan brothers for that matter. Furthermore, they had made a fool of him by scorning his hospitality and generosity to throw in their lot with the outlaws in the wilderness. Let them now pay the price.

He climbed the steps of the gallows to make himself seen and heard by everyone present. "Good people, I sympathize with what you are saying, but I am powerless to do anything about it. You have all seen the proclamation yourselves, and have known long before now that every single outlaw, without exception, would be hanged when captured. It's the law. I don't have the authority to change it. The hangings must proceed."

No one in the crowd had the presence of mind at that moment to remind Stanford that it was he himself who had been the author of the proclamation, and that he did indeed therefore have the power and authority to change it if he chose to do so. They were stunned into disbelieving silence.

Stanford knew that he had to get it all over with quickly, before the concern of the crowd escalated into outright hostility. He had committed himself. He couldn't back down now, no matter what. Abandoning the pomp and ritual that had accompanied the executions of Foley and Shaheen, he ordered that Duffy go first.

The sixteen-year-old boy faced the crowd with a dignity that neither of the two grown men who had gone before him had shown. Although his eyes were still reddened by the tears that had dried up hours earlier, the dread and fear that he felt inside did not otherwise show on his face.

The chaplain, who despite his calling had been as glad as everybody else to have seen Foley and Shaheen dispatched so readily, was moved by the sight of the young boy. He felt tears welling up in his own eyes. Although in his position he could raise no objection, he too knew that it was a mortal sin for this boy to hanged.

"Father, I'm afraid. Will it hurt much?" The boy's clear blue eyes pleaded for reassurance. The protestant chaplain made no effort to explain to him that he was not a Roman Catholic priest.

"No, my son. It will all be over before you know it. You won't feel a thing."

"And what about the flames? They told me I'll burn in hell forever for what I've done."

"Don't worry about that either, my son. There'll be no flames where you're going. Only peace and love and sunshine. You'll never know hunger or cold or suffering again, and you'll be with all the loved ones you ever knew."

"And what about Paddy? Will he be there too?"

The chaplain made no effort to try to hold back the tears that now flowed freely down his face. "Yes, yes, my son. Paddy will be there with you and you'll never be parted again."

"Ah, Father. It sounds grand, don't it?" The boy's sudden smile tore the chaplain's soul apart.

A few seconds later Duffy plunged into the wonderful world that the chaplain had just described to him. And not long afterward, fifteen-year-old Paddy O'Brien joined him, entrenching for eternity the friendship that had started in Ireland three years earlier.

The crowd was transfixed. Somewhere a woman wailed. Fathers and mothers gripped their small children to their breasts. Nobody moved when Stanford gave the order for the bodies of Foley, Shaheen, Duffy, and O'Brien to be taken out to sea and dumped, where the sharks and the dogfish would feast on their flesh and bones.

"Noooo!" The heartfelt cry from somewhere in the crowd brought everyone to their senses. The startled settlers parted to let Father Fabian through as he strode forward toward the gallows. He had watched the entire proceeding, as paralyzed as everybody else by what he had witnessed. He was heartbroken and devastated by the knowledge that it was his own misguided act of kindness that had ultimately led to the boys' executions.

Stanford stood stock-still as the young priest approached

him. Father Fabian didn't waver.

"I'll take the two boys."

"Indeed?" Stanford's lips curled in scorn. "By whose authority do you propose to do that? They're outlaws, just like the others, and only got what they deserved."

A low growl started to emanate from the crowd, swelling the air with the threat of violence. The settlers were awakening from their stupor. Sensing the menace of the moment, Stanford smiled at Father Fabian. He already had his victory.

"Take them. They're yours. But remember this, priest, I know what you've done, and I can come for you anytime I want to. Don't ever forget it."

And he stalked away, leaving Father Fabian to his task. When the young priest gathered the lifeless body of Duffy into his arms and turned to walk along the beach, away from the gallows and towards Peter's Brook, many of the settlers started to follow him. He stopped them.

"Stay here. I'll be back for the other one."

He proceeded alone until he reached the mouth of the river. Then he followed the footpath through the woods that led to the barrens. The slight body of Duffy felt almost weightless in his arms. He progressed through the clearing in the woods, where Hannah Martin watched him pass, and continued his journey until he arrived at the fringe of the wilderness area. And there, under the spreading branches of the Fairy Tree, whose new leaves were only now beginning to burst into life, he laid the boy's body.

He retraced his steps back to the beach where the crowd still waited. Nobody had left. At least two dozen settlers had formed a protective ring around the body of Paddy O'Brien in case Stanford decided to change his mind. The bodies of Foley and Shaheen were already gone.

Father Fabian made his second trip to the Fairy Tree, this time carrying the even lighter O'Brien. There, he rearranged the two bodies as best he could, closing their unseeing eyes, folding their arms across their chests, even making some attempt at combing their unruly and unkempt hair. He wept openly, his soul shattered, as he said the last rites over the bodies of the two boys whose only true moments of happiness on earth had been those spent among the outlaws in the wilderness. Then he walked out onto the open barrens, praying that Kerrivan and the others were still somewhere out there and would see him.

Before the evening sun slipped below the horizon, the bodies of Brian Duffy and Paddy O'Brien were collected from beneath the Fairy Tree. And before darkness settled over the Southern Shore, they were in the ground at the base of the Butterpot mountain.

twentyeight

I ronically, it took the deaths of Brian Duffy and Paddy O'Brien to trigger the change in the relationship between the settlers of the area and the outlaws in the wilderness that would take place over the ensuing months. When, after the hangings, the spectators had filed past the corpses of the two boys, they became painfully aware of their small undernourished bodies, their pitifully thin arms and legs, and their faces, still childlike despite the grotesque distortion caused by the noose. As they viewed the small bodies dressed in ragged and torn clothing, the settlers could not believe that these were two of the outlaws that they had feared so long. They were not much more than children.

In the following days and weeks, the executions, especially those of O'Brien and Duffy, were the main topic of conversation along the coast. Many of the settlers who had witnessed the gruesome event were still troubled by the sight of the bodies of the two boys jerking and twitching on the end of the rope for what seemed like an eternity before finally becoming still. Worse still, some of them had brought their own young children along to see the grim spectacle. As they talked about it amongst themselves and pondered it in their own minds, many of them began to develop a degree of empathy for the outlaws and a deepening distrust and dislike for Lieutenant Stanford and his men. They wanted no more hangings. Many of them, even though they could not condone the actions of the outlaws and still felt uncomfortable having them in the vicinity, came to the realization like Father Fabian that the wild men out on the barrens might not be monsters and ogres after all, but mere mortals like themselves. Perhaps, they concluded, Kerrivan and the others could yet be somewhat redeemed if someone cared enough to see things from their perspective and tried to extend a sympathetic hand. The more Christian and charitable among them now often included the outlaws in their prayers. Perhaps in time, if the outlaws ceased their lawless ways, they might even be able to forgive them.

Many settlers, especially those in Renews where the hangings had taken place, no longer reported missing items, which they assumed had been taken by the outlaws, to Stanford or to anyone else. Some even got into the habit of occasionally placing items of food and clothing in judicious locations where the outlaws would be sure to find them.

And then one day in late August, another event occurred that would cement the new relationship between the settlers and Kerrivan and the other members of his outlaw band, and eventually lead to the exodus of the men out of the wilderness and into the villages and hamlets of the Southern Shore.

A group of seven children from Renews had taken advantage of the fine weather to go berry picking. Despite the admonitions of their mothers not to venture out onto the open barrens, as the day wore on the children gradually gravitated toward the taboo wilderness area where they knew that the blueberries and partridgeberries would be bigger and more plentiful. Encouraged and led by two of the older children, the group could not resist the temptation to move further and further out into the open space. Even though they knew they were disobeying their parents, they also knew that if they returned with their pails full few questions would be asked.

After being there only a relatively short time, the children were forced to abandon their berry picking expedition and head for home when a heavy dense fog suddenly settled over the area. They were partway back along the path that ran beside Peter's Brook before they realized that the two O'Grady children, Marcie and her brother, Willie, who had been lagging behind the others, were nowhere to be seen. They tried to retrace their steps back to the barrens, but by this time they could see only a few yards ahead of them. Their frantic calling into the fog brought no response, and after more than fifteen minutes of fruitless effort, the children, now worried and frightened themselves, decided that they had better go back to the settlement and get some grownups to come and find their friends.

The massive search that took place for the rest of that day and the following two days failed to turn up the lost boy and girl, aged four and six respectively. Hampered by the thick fog that hugged the ground for the entire period, the feverish efforts of the men and women of Renews and those from the other nearby settlements who had come to help in the search, were in vain. Finally, on the third day the fog lifted a little, yet there was still no sign of Marcie and Willie O'Grady. The searchers sadly concluded that the two small children must have fallen into one of the barrens' many ponds and bog-holes, and that their bodies must be somewhere in their murky depths. After another day of futile searching in a heavy rain that sometimes fell in torrents and certain that they had covered every inch of ground, they had given up any hope that the children would ever be found alive. If they had not drowned, they would surely by this time have died of exposure. Some even believed that the outlaws had taken them. Thomas O'Grady and his wife, Mary, were devastated by the loss of two of their six children, their most precious possessions. They blamed no one but themselves for having allowed it to happen. The rest of Renews and the surrounding area shared their sorrow.

Then, two days after the search had been abandoned and the weather finally cleared, the people of Renews were astounded when a tall, fierce, blond-haired man with piercing blue eyes, walked into their settlement carrying a tiny boy in his arms and leading a small girl by the hand. Scarcely able to believe what they were witnessing, they followed him in silence as he made his way toward the Presbytery. Before he reached there, Kerrivan was met by Father Fabian, into whose waiting arms he deposited the sleeping Willie O'Grady and his tired but now safe sister, Marcie.

Father Fabian was as flabbergasted as everyone else by what was happening. It was the first time he had met face to face the man in whom he had taken such an interest for so many years. Kerrivan was almost exactly as he had pictured him in his mind, although perhaps a little taller and thinner.

"Where in God's name did you find them?" he asked.

Kerrivan appeared to be oblivious to the crowd of people

around him, focusing only on the priest in front of him. He wondered at the youthfulness of the only person in the area who had ever tried to help him and the other members of his band in their dire existence in the wilderness.

"I came across them on the barrens. The boy was barely alive when I found him, and the girl not much better. With the bad weather, I thought it best to take them to the mountain and try to get them warm and dry. I had to wait until it was fit enough to bring them here. I feared they might have perished on the way."

By then the distraught Thomas and Mary O'Grady had made their appearance and taken Marcie and Willie into their custody, rejoicing and weeping unashamedly at having their children restored to them. Before either of them heard the full story and had a chance to thank Kerrivan, the leader of the outlaw band was gone. Without saying another word, he had simply turned away from Father Fabian and the crowd, and started to make his way back to the mountain. No one made any attempt to follow him.

twentynine

One morning early in the following spring Hannah Martin awoke to the realization that she was carrying Peter Kerrivan's child. For more than a week she had been feeling strangely off, especially in the mornings, never quite able to figure out what was wrong with her. It had not dawned on her until now that it might be because she was pregnant. And she did not know what to make of it.

Her initial reaction was one of disbelief and incredulity that she, after all these years and at her age, was carrying inside her another human being. She was frightened at the thought and her mind swirled with concerns and apprehension. How could she provide for a child and look after it in her own dire circumstances there in the clearing in the woods? What if she got sick again herself or something went wrong with the birth itself and there was no one there to help her, or even more importantly, to help the baby? What if her child died?

She calculated that the baby would arrive sometime in the fall, probably October, which presented yet another set of problems. That was a very critical time of the year for her. It was when she had to harvest her potatoes and vegetable crops and get them properly stored for the winter, grueling work that taxed her strength and energy each year. Her very existence depended on it. In her condition, would she be capable of doing what had to be done?

Kerrivan did not find out for another three weeks. Even though he now came to see her at least once a week, Hannah hesitated to tell him until she was absolutely certain herself. She wondered how he would react. When she finally told him, he was as amazed as she herself had been. Still, the concept of fatherhood was foreign to the man who had spent most of his life among hardened criminals and fugitives with no sense of responsibility toward anyone or anything other than their own welfare and survival, and it would be a long time before the fact that he would soon be the father of a child would fully register in his mind.

As the weeks and months of summer passed, Hannah's worries and concerns were gradually dispelled by the knowledge that someday soon she would be able to hold in her arms the child that she now felt stirring inside her as she went about her work, and be able to feel the softness of its flesh and the warmth of its tiny body. And her days were filled with wonder. Each little kick sent a thrill through her, and on a few occasions she was even certain she had felt the unborn child hiccuping. She wondered whether it was a boy or a girl, and what it would look like. She realized that she didn't really care, all that mattered was that it be born alive and healthy. She made a promise that she would look after herself as best she could, knowing that the state of her own health would be vitally important to that of her unborn child.

Having gotten over her initial anxiety, the prospect of motherhood now sat well with her. The promise of someone to share her life, as poor as it was, and upon whom she could focus her love and affection and perhaps repay the years of love and caring that Aunt Beatrice had bestowed upon her as a child in Harbour Grace, brought a new purpose to her existence. She was happier and more contented than she had been in many years.

Father Fabian visited her twice during the early months of her pregnancy. At first she had hesitated to tell him, and when she finally did so she realized that her condition was probably obvious to him by then anyway. She had been unable to read anything in his reaction, either recrimination or sanction. His true feelings were important to her. She was gratified by the fact that before he left, the prayer he shared with her included a plea to God, "to bless and look after this woman and her unborn child."

And then one day in mid-August as she was walking beside Peter's Brook looking for ferns and wild-flowers, her sense of well-being was abruptly invaded by the unbeckoned admission that she had unconsciously or otherwise been suppressing something of great importance. It had been there all along in the back of her mind, yet she knew now that from the moment she had first known she was pregnant she had avoided facing the fact that the child she was carrying had been conceived in sin and would be born a bastard, something against which her strong Protestant upbringing rebelled. Her happiness and contentment were now overshadowed by guilt and the knowledge that she had sinned yet again in the eyes of the Lord. And she didn't know what to do. She remembered a young girl in Harbour Grace whose child had been born out of wedlock, and the church would not even acknowledge the father's name on the baptism register. Even worse, she recalled that both the mother and the child had been marked from that day as objects of scorn and ridicule, sometimes pitied but scarcely welcomed anywhere in the community.

With the birth of her own child only a few weeks away, her days became a mixture of emotions that ran the gamut from joy whenever the child let her know that it would soon be ready to face the world to sadness and pain whenever she thought about the circumstances of its conception. Finally, with the inner strength and conviction that she had always possessed, she decided that she had to do something. It was too late to do anything about the fact that the child had been conceived in sin. Yet perhaps there was still time to ensure that the child, once born, would be reared in an environment suitable to the Lord and compatible with her own religious beliefs. And for the first time since coming from Harbour Grace many years earlier, she left the clearing in the woods and ventured into the settlement of Renews to see Father Fabian.

When the young priest heard Hannah's plea and accompanied her back to the clearing in the woods, where Kerrivan was waiting, he knew that the act he was about to perform could never be sanctioned by the Vatican and the Roman Catholic Church, and that he himself might be severely reprimanded as a consequence, possibly even dismissed. The unborn child was illegitimate, conceived out of wedlock by a reclusive woman shunned by the entire Roman Catholic population of the area in which she lived. Worse still, she was a Protestant, and the father, a convicted murderer and a fugitive from the law, was an atheist at best. And on top of all that, the child would be born into an environment of isolation and poverty that no child of any race, color or creed anywhere deserved.

He knew, however, in his heart and soul, that the union of Hannah Martin and Peter Kerrivan was right in the eyes of God. And there in the afternoon sun, with no one to witness except the birds, and perhaps the hovering spirits of Brian Duffy, Paddy O'Brien and Styles, the Snitch, he made them man and wife.

That night he slept in his bed in the Presbytery as soundly and as peacefully as ever before in the certainty that his actions that day had found favor with the Lord – and that God himself would guide the paths of the Kerrivans and their child from that day onward.

thirty

The first ship to arrive in Ferryland Harbour in the spring of 1756 brought with it Lieutenant Stanford's long awaited recall to England. Within a month he was gone, leaving behind him the unfinished business of the outlaws in the wilderness. Sadly, he did not leave behind any friends. At the end of his fourteen year stay in the Plantation, he could not point to a single individual that he could call a true friend or companion. The few men with whom he had once associated had been alienated by his bizarre and erratic behavior during the latter years of his term. Everyone was glad to see him go. By then even his wife and his two daughters were virtual strangers to him.

The man who came to replace him, Naval Governor Myles Grimes, was a very different type of individual from his predecessor. Like Stanford, he was a disciplinarian and a stickler for rules and regulations. But the resemblance to Stanford ended there. As a naval officer, he had always commanded his men in a manner that demanded their admiration and respect, if not love. For Grimes, a four-year stint in Ferryland would be a satisfactory conclusion to a long and distinguished career that had previously taken him to Australia, America, and now Newfoundland.

Two months after his arrival, he was visited in the garrison one morning by a contingent of settlers from Renews and some of the other nearby settlements with one of the most unusual requests that he had ever heard. The settlers were there to seek a pardon for the outlaws in the wilderness, the scourge that had harassed and pillaged them for almost six years. The leader of the group presenting the petition was a Roman Catholic priest who introduced himself as Father Fabian O'Donnell. The other members of the contingent seemed content to let the young priest do most of the talking, content to chime in occasionally to support him in what he was saying.

Grimes listened with great interest to what Father O'Donnell and the others had to tell him. He had already been brought up to date on the past activities of Kerrivan, Finn, and the other members of the outlaw gang, and was aware of the havoc that they had wrought upon the area over the years. He was puzzled by the fact that these settlers were now not only willing to forgive the outlaws for all that they had done, but were even willing to accept them into their communities and their homes. Some of them, he was told, had in fact already formed friendships of a sort with the outlaws.

Sensing the earnestness of their plea, he found himself involuntarily siding with their request, a strange position for him to take, he knew, in such a situation. New to the area and recognizing that this was an opportunity to establish an early rapport with the settlers, who appeared to be united in their request, the wily veteran officer wondered if there was some way he could meet them halfway.

After due consideration, knowing full well that he was needlessly putting himself out on a limb, he told them, "I'll tell you what I'll do. I can't grant an outright pardon to any of these men. I simply don't have the legal authority to pardon crimes, whatever they might be, that were committed in other jurisdictions. No matter what they've done since coming here, their original crimes, or so I am led to believe, were committed in England or Ireland or other places far from here. Therefore I can't do anything about them. And I don't know if you as a group represent the wishes of the other residents of the area. I'll have to give them the opportunity to protest this petition if they so desire. But if they don't, I promise you this – I won't be the one to initiate any raids against the outlaws, and I'll turn a blind eye to their existence here as long as they behave themselves and there is no further trouble. It's the best I can do."

It was enough. When Father Fabian told Kerrivan what had transpired at the garrison, the outlaw leader pledged to put a stop to the band's harassment of Renews and the other settlements along the shore, a promise that for the most part he would live up to. While, over the ensuing months, possessions of the settlers' still occasionally went missing and there were still a few minor incidents involving some members of the outlaw band, Kerrivan, Finn, and the others made a determined effort to keep the peace. Instead of trying to continue to survive in the wilderness by theft and intimidation, they turned to trading with the settlers and offering themselves for odd jobs of work whenever possible and otherwise managing to live by more civilized means. It was a beneficial arrangement for both parties. The settlers readily exchanged items of food and clothing for the fresh caribou meat and hides that the outlaws brought with them, and for the first time, the outlaws were able to acquire an ample supply of shot and powder for their muskets, and an occasional jug of rum or ale.

Gradually, the relationship between the outlaws and the residents of this stretch of the Southern Shore softened to the point that the fear and hostility of the past all but disappeared. The increasingly frequent appearances of the men from the wilderness in their communities no longer caused the settlers any great concern or anxiety. In the space of another year or so, the outlaws would begin to leave their lair at the base of the Butterpot mountain once and for all, and one by one blend into the settlements of the Southern Shore, bringing the curtain down on the final chapter of their extended exile in the wilderness. The Society of Masterless Men had run its course.

thirtyone

The hovel in the clearing had long since been leveled to the ground and taken away and burned. In its place stood the fine little cottage that Hannah Martin (now Hannah Kerrivan) had envisaged when Ned Madigan had taken her away with him from Harbour Grace so many years earlier. The weed-free potato garden was well composted with a layer of rotting caplin, and the healthy stalks that rose from the ground were an indication of the fine crop of potatoes that grew beneath them. The smaller garden adjacent to it, also obviously well tended, contained turnips, carrots, beet and cabbage, and in a small section at its extreme edge, a mixture of herbs and colorful flowers. A large stack of fire-logs and a neat pile of split junks lay ready for burning. A small ditch that had been dug from the brook to the house brought a constant trickle of fresh water to a stone cistern, where it could be readily fetched without having to walk all the way to the brook each time it was needed.

Inside, Hannah brought Peter his morning tea as he sat at the kitchen table. On some days, like this one, Peter was confused and often didn't know where he was, or what he was supposed to be doing. Sometimes Hannah wondered if he even knew her at such moments. When he was like this, Hannah made sure that he was properly dressed, washed, and that he took his meals when he was supposed to.

But on the day that someone from the settlement had come and brought him the news that a large naval frigate called the *Fortress* had run onto the rocks off Bay Bulls and been battered to pieces, his mind was as clear as it had ever been in his lifetime. The name of the ship, long forgotten, brought back a flood of memories, and he sat for a long time at the kitchen table reliving the events of the past sixty years as vividly as if they had happened only yesterday.

He was seventy-one years of age, and his once tall and muscular body was now bent and thin. His joints, especially his knees, ached continuously from the arthritis and rheumatism that he blamed on his years of living out in the wilderness. He found cold, damp days the worst. However, his once blond hair, now almost snow white, was still as full as it had ever been, and his blue eyes stared from their sockets with the same intensity of his earlier years.

Despite his aches and pains, and his periods of confusion, his life with Hannah was good. When their son, Peter (for Hannah would consider no other name for her firstborn child) brought his own children to visit, he felt blessed beyond anything he had ever hoped for. He took immense pleasure from the sight of the three blond-haired, blue-eyed children, two boys and a girl, playing and romping around the house or outside in the clearing. He finally knew the happiness and contentment that Nanny Williams had prophesied for him that night in London fifty-five years earlier when he had confronted her about his destiny.

When he finally emerged from his reverie, he looked for a long time at the woman who sat sewing on the other side of the kitchen table. Her body was as gaunt and bent as his, and the joints of her long, bony fingers were gnarled and disfigured by arthritis much worse than his own. She held her work so close to her eyes, in order to see what she was doing, that some of the cloth that she was sewing sometimes brushed against her face.

And as he looked at her, so absorbed in her work that she was unaware of his gaze, his heart swelled with the love that had grown stronger and deeper every day since he had first held her in the clearing in the woods so long ago.

His tea was cold, too cold to drink, and he rose from his chair and went outside and emptied it onto the ground. It didn't matter. It would be one of his last, for within a fortnight he was gone, passing away quietly in his sleep early one morning as he lay beside Hannah in their bed. Without any tears or lamentations to betray the overwhelming sense of loss that she felt inside, Hannah had fetched her son and Father Fabian, and together they buried him.

And, as if by design so that they wouldn't be parted for too long, Hannah herself died a few weeks later as she sat in her chair next to the fire. Her son, Peter, found her there, her hands folded as if in prayer and her face composed in peace and tranquility. With her family all present, Father Fabian, her long-time friend and benefactor, gave her a full Roman Catholic burial despite the fact that she had always remained a Protestant, and laid her to rest beside her husband in the clearing in the woods.

Peter's death brought closure to the story of the Society of Masterless Men. Most of the others who had been members of his band in the wilderness had long since integrated into society. Many had blended into the settlements along the Southern Shore, like Finn, who had moved all the way down to Trepassey, where he married, raised six children, and started a successful chandlers operation. Some left the Shore altogether, mostly to go to St. John's, and a few made their way back to England and Ireland.

For the Shannahan brothers, the siren call of Ireland had still been too strong, and, despite the price on their heads, they returned to their ancestral home. Unfortunately, the lust for freedom from their British overlords still burned as fiercely as ever in their Irish breasts, and they became embroiled in a yet another failed uprising. This time their English judges were not as lenient, and the two brothers paid with their lives.

Father Fabian, the beloved little priest of the Renews Parish, continued his work of love among the settlers of Fermeuse, Aquaforte, Renews, and Cappahayden until he was found dead in his bed one morning by the young priest who had been sent over from Waterford to assist him only a few months earlier.

Lieutenant Philip Stanford, following his recall to England, was sent to America to help the British forces there put down the unrest and rebellion that would shortly afterward escalate into the American Revolution. There, in 1775, he was felled on the battlefield of Lexington by a ball from the musket of an American patriot. He was one of the first British soldiers to die during the eight-year war that would result in the United

States of America's independence from British rule. Ironically, upon his arrival there, he had found the American patriots to be even more uncultured and churlish than the settlers of the Ferryland Plantation and the other settlements of the Southern Shore of Newfoundland.

James Kilfoy, for his role in the sequence of events that had transpired, did indeed focus upon himself the attention and recognition that he craved. It wasn't quite what he hoped for, however, as instead of endearing him to the other settlers in the area, it further alienated him until he eventually left the Southern Shore altogether and went to St. John's. For many years afterward the term "Kilfoy" was used in Renews and the other nearby settlements in much the same way as the name Benedict Arnold would be referred to in the fledgling United States of America.

The Butterpot mountain still stands serene in the wilderness, as pristine and pure as it has ever been. There is no lasting evidence to indicate that Kerrivan's band of lawless men had once lived there. The birds and the small animals once again have the mountain to themselves. But if you happened to be there in the soft twilight of some perfect day, you might hear, as a handful of people have claimed down through the years, the joyful laughter of youthful voices. And perhaps, if you looked close enough, as an even smaller number have claimed, you might catch a fleeting glimpse of two boys as they frolicked and chased each other through the shrubbery and goowithy at the base of the mountain.

epilogue

The foregoing story is based on the legend of the Society of Masterless Men,[5] a band of lawless renegades who lived in the wilderness of the Southern Shore of the Avalon Peninsula in the mid to late 1700's. Their full story, if known, would undoubtedly be much more interesting and exciting than the fictional account I have tried to present.

There is little hard and fast evidence to support the legend of the Masterless Men. Much of what we know about them stems from The Oral History of Ferryland compiled by Howard Morry and John Hawkins in the 1950's. Well-known Newfoundland author, Harold Horwood, in a subsequent article in The Newfoundland Quarterly, expanded upon the works of Morry and Hawkins, and a brief reference to Kerrivan and his band of outlaws is made in The Boat Who Wouldn't Float by Farley Mowatt. According to these sources, a man of Irish descent named Peter Kerrivan, believed to have been seized by a press-gang and forced into service in the British Navy, deserted from his ship in Ferryland in 1750 and led a number of other men into the area known as the Butterpot Barrens, where he and his companions lived for an undetermined number of years. It is not known how many others accompanied him, or their names, but is thought that they were, like himself, deserters from the navy or escaped prisoners or indentured men who had run away from the nearby plantations. While the exact location of their hideout

---

[5] The term Masterless Men was generally employed in Newfoundland at the time in reference to indentured apprentices or seasonal workers who had run away from their masters, or were deserters from the navy. In Newfoundland folklore, however, it has almost exclusively been associated with Peter Kerrivan and his band of lawless men.

has never been conclusively determined, it is generally believed to have been in the vicinity of the Butterpot Mountain,[6] about nine miles inland from Ferryland. There they lived in crude shacks roughly constructed from spruce poles, bark, and boughs, the only building materials available to them in the area.

According to the legend, they survived in the wilderness by hunting and fishing, and supplementing their needs and wants by occasionally raiding the nearby settlements of Ferryland, Fermeuse, Aquaforte, Renews, and Cappahayden. Over a period of years, Kerrivan and his original compatriots were joined by many other men, most of them runaway indentured servants or fishermen who preferred a life of exile in the wilderness to the cruel and brutal treatment they received from their merchant fishing masters, and the band eventually grew to a considerable size. As time passed and their numbers increased, the outlaws also traded, albeit surreptitiously, with the settlers, exchanging furs, hides, and meat for staples such as tea, flour, and salt. They became expert woodsmen and hunters, and the great caribou herd that existed on the Avalon Peninsula at that time provided them with a constant supply of food.

For many years, Kerrivan and his men avoided capture by the naval authorities who frequently came searching for them, becoming almost folk heroes to many of the settlers in the area. There is some indication that their pursuers were more often than not foiled by a complex of false trails that the Masterless Men had designed to divert them away from the real location of their wilderness village. From their vantage point on the Butterpot Mountain, Kerrivan and his men had a clear view of the surrounding area and could easily spot any force of men coming toward them. There is also some suggestion that they had allies in the settlements who would sometimes warn them of such impending raids. When attacked, they would simply melt into the westernmost wilderness and wait there until the authorities left again. On at least one occasion, however, the log

---

[6] Not to be confused with another small mountain also called the Butterpot which is located near Holyrood, Conception Bay, and from which the Butterpot Provincial Park derives its name.

huts that they left behind were discovered by their pursuers and burned and their contents destroyed.

Still, despite their best efforts to shield and protect themselves from the authorities, it is known for certain that at least four of the outlaws were caught and hanged from the yardarm of a naval frigate in Ferryland Harbour. It is believed that at least two of them, if not all four, were indentured Irish youths from nearby settlements who had escaped from their fishing merchant masters to join Kerrivan's band.

The exact length of their stay in the wilderness is also unknown. There is some evidence, scant and inconclusive though it may be, to suggest that some of the men may still have been living there in the latter part of the eighteenth century (much longer than the period of time depicted in my own fictional account). This assumption is based mainly on court records that show that a man named Thomas Kerrivan, possibly a son or relative of Peter Kerrivan, was among a large group of Irish renegades arrested for rioting in 1791 and subsequently deported to Ireland. Also, the overt practice of Roman Catholicism and celebration of Mass in my story is a bit early. It was not until 1784 that, "full liberty of conscience and the free exercise of such modes of worship as are not prohibited by same ...,"[7] was proclaimed. Prior to that date the gathering of Roman Catholics to worship and celebrate Mass was prohibited by law, and was performed in secret by itinerant priests who moved from settlement to settlement. The usual penalty for defying this law was a substantial fine for those attending and the burning of the houses or fishing rooms where such illegal gatherings were held.

As the eighteenth century drew to a close and the laws of Newfoundland relaxed to the extent that men were permitted to own land and work for themselves without being bound to the fishing merchants or planters, the outlaws from the Butterpot Barrens gradually left the wilderness area and integrated into the coastal settlements that they had once raided and pillaged, where they settled down, married local women, and raised families. It is believed, however, that

---

[7] Extract from edict issued by Governor J. Campbell on October 28,1784.

Kerrivan himself, who supposedly sired four sons and a number of daughters, never returned to civilization but lived out his remaining years in his wilderness home.

Could it be that some of the names inscribed on the ancient headstones of the older graveyards of the Southern Shore, particularly those along the stretch of coastline between Ferryland and Cappahayden, are those of men who had at one time been members of the Society of Masterless Men, or their direct descendants? Or do some of the crumbling tombstones on which the original wording is no longer legible mark the graves where their bones are interred? It is possible, perhaps even likely. Unfortunately, there are no definitive markings on any of them or any other concrete evidence of any kind to support this notion – or to refute it. For all traces of Kerrivan and the others who had once comprised the Society of Masterless Men appear to have died with them.